MONTANA

MONTANA

HIGH RISE AND HANDSOME

A LAND WHERE COWBOYS AND INDIANS ONCE ROAMED AND
WHERE DOCTORS, LAWYERS, CEOS, INTERNET INDUSTRIALISTS, AND
AGRABUSINESS PERSONS NOW JOG, DO YOGA, EAT VEGAN, AND
REALLY GET INTO THE GREAT OUTDOORS.

Serena Sofia Flighfish

To order additional copies of this book, contact:
Xlibris Corporation
1-888-795-4274
www.Xlibris.com
Orders@Xlibris.com
31778

Contents

OTHER BOOKS BY THE AUTHOR

FERAGAMO IN ELECTRIC COBALT BLUE
DINING WITH NORTHWEST DIVINITIES
HIGHWIRE DANCING INSIDE THE BELTWAY
LINGERIE FIRECRACKER STORIES
WHAT THE RABBIT SAW

Those who spend their life suffering for the sins of the world
would do the world better if they laughed with us over
a glass of wine, good bread, and a fine French cheese.

SHANE! COME BACK SHANE! SHANE!

For those of us who grew up in New York, Boston, Philadelphia, Cleveland, Atlanta, or Chicago, the American West was the wild, wild West—an American frontier cluttered with gun-toting gun-fighting towns, gold claims, cattle drives, sod busters, and pioneer wagon trains. Sheepherders and cattle ranchers didn't cotton to each other, dealers from the bottom of the deck got what's comin' to 'im, fellars could get bushwhacked if they weren't curful, and the quick-draw shootouts were at High Noon. And all this was going on in 1955 when everybody's fathers traded in the Second World War Chevrolet, Ford, or Plymouth for a new brand new Chevrolet, Ford, or Plymouth with tail fins the size of cattle horns.

We knew all about the West because every Friday night the family watched a double bill at the local movie theatre of John Wayne and Alan Ladd taking down bad guys like Billy the Kid when nobody was killing Indians. The American West was filled with purple mountains majesty, red deserts, and rattlesnakes as thick as Roy Rodgers and the Cisco Kid hog-tied together.

For Matthew, Mark, Luke, and John, and Mary, Mary, Mary, Martha, and Marie, every birthday wish was the same. They wanted a million dollars in gold and a horse, though they could never figure out whether the cost of the horse should be deducted from the million or its purchase price should be in addition to it. And it had to be just a horse, because growing up in New York, Boston, Philadelphia, Cleveland, Atlanta, or Chicago, they did not know an Appaloosa from a Lippizaner. They never got the money or the horse, but their fathers did exchange the Admiral 12' b & w in the living room for an RCA 21" color tv in the den, and soon the screen was filled with *Gunsmoke*, *Have Gun Will Travel*, *The Rifleman*, *Bonanza*, and other such proofs of the reality of a non-existent American West—past, present and future.

But as the wagon wheel turns, birthday followed birthday, high school followed grammar, and then college awarded a degree and sent the young packing to where else but the megalopolises of Denver, Houston, and Oklahoma City to sell insurance or manage a K-Mart. Some were more fortunate, for with their diploma in hand they ended up working in a Montana that is high, wide and handsome, the last best place, the wide-open spaces, and Big Sky Country. Winters in Montana are glacial, as are the two weeks of spring and fall, but nevertheless, it is a wondrous place, and sometime during their first decade of residency, they saw a cowboy.

They saw the cowboy at the High Plains Shopping Mall which looks just like a New York, Chicago, Los Angeles, or Austin, Texas, shopping mall—a bit smaller perhaps, but stocked with the same Old Navy, Gap, Borders, J.C. Penney's, Macy's and Sears. They could tell he was a cowboy because he wore a ten-gallon hat and he kept riding up and down in the glass-fronted elevator. Then there was the sheepherder who they knew was a sheepherder because he smelled of sheep and he could not refrain from sheepishly glancing at the lingeried manikins at Victoria's Secret.

There are no gunfights at OK Corral because there ain't no OK Corral, though maybe its remains lie somewhere buried under the MacDonald's, Burger King, Wendy's, or Sonic's parking lot. Montanans know that even if a river filled with brown trout and rainbows runs through it, so, too, do several hundred miles of expressways. Maybe there was a time when pickup trucks with rifle rack, rifle with scope for deer, elk, and bear hunting, and big ugly dog in the bed ruled. Now, Montana is home to New York and California ex-patriots who have traded their Lexus, Mercedes, and Cadillac sedans for a Lexus SUV, Mercedes SUV, and Cadillac Escalade. Then there are the doctors, lawyers, and a vast assortment of middle management, some transplants and some native sons and daughters, who reject the Lexus and Beemer and opt for a Subaru and tofu existence. Avant-garde artists, the latest versions of Christian fundamentalists and neo-Nazis, and hermits pretending to be mountain men, all searching for inspiration or maybe even divine intervention live here.

Yes, there still are far far too many people in New York, Detroit, Chicago, Berlin, Paris, Tokyo and Moscow who believe those tall tales about the wild, wild West, and all that can be done with such people is to replace their beloved fictions with a whole new set of fairy tales. Stories must be fashioned that present a reality that never existed in an Old West that did not exist yesterday and does not exist today. New myths, fantasies, fairy tales and tall tales are now in order, since the truth never convinced anybody.

Unlike a neat, tidy short story or novel, reality can begin anywhere it chooses, then wander off only to show up later somewhere else as somewhat familiar while somehow different. Reality can appear out of nowhere for no reason at all and it can end not by ending but by simply fading out. Destinations are not reached, the signposts do not point, and it is all a jumble of highways and byways, roadways and crossroads, side streets and alleys, trail, track, and path. All we have is a bit of common sense and luck to guide us through the maze.

The following stories are about Montana; some are about life in Montana, and some are about Montana lives—biographical sketches of real people whose lives are framed by towns like Two Dot, Three Forks, and Scobey, and cities like Butte, Bozeman, Missoula, Helena, and Billings. True, some of these people have since died and others have not yet been born, but lots of people are like that. Nor should one suppose that the people herein are in reality fictitious; rather, they are no less real than who they are in some yearbook, credit agency or social service organization file folder. Those who have been closest to the author long ago realized that her existence too has been fiction, with the exception of the Fourth of July in 1987.*

The following stories compare favorably to *The Iliad* and *The Odyssey*, the latter recently presented so convincingly by Leonardo DiCaprio, Brad Pitt, Kate Winslet, and Charlize Theron. Though neither as erotic nor lascivious as a Hollywood cinematic triumph, and that is a shame, Montana's montage has been just as neurotic. Montanans are thankful that they have had more than their fair share of sexual encounters, but unlike St. Augustine or Rush Limbaugh, they have not felt the need to derive from such either a theology of salvation or unforgivable ignorance.

The author has undertaken publication of the following stories not because she has anything insightful to say or that some fortunate reader could learn valuable lessons from this work, but because she is moved to review Montana lives which without a second thought were not spent in the service of others or working for the greater good. If the author is convinced of anything, it is that people with a highly developed moral sense or in possession of a book of divinely revealed revelations, only have made matters worse. The author adds that her dog recently ran off and joined the circus, which, though many people would look down upon such behavior, has brought the author and the dog nothing but joy. The dog is far happier riding on the backs of horses than taking paw-blistering treks through the strip malls, shopping centers, and vast Wal-Mart parking lots that have so recently civilized *Montana: High, Wide and Handsome*, *The Big Sky*, *A River Runs Through It*, and *The Last Best Place*.

However, it is entirely possible that as the reader wanders through the following collage he or she will conclude that this is not about Montana at all, and who is the author to disagree? This is said because the author has learned

---

* As any post-modern scholar will report, that a text has an author is a completely unnecessary supposition. Therefore, the stories in the following pages should be thought of as a random downloading from various Internet sites.

through many unfortunate experiences that if you want people to agree with you, you should make yourself agreeable and affirm other people's observations no matter how inaccurate, misguided, absurd, or simply wrong. Therefore, the reader is right to conclude that what follows is not about Montana at all, but rather a loose bunching of observations about people, places, and events that do not exist, and even if they did, any sane person would simply cross the street and pretend not to notice.

Montana is not a fictional land, but one filled with absolutely real unrealities. If this is difficult to understand, just consider all those John Wayne Alan Ladd Gary Cooper Clint Eastwood Jack Elam Westerns that made the wild West a reality not only to millions of Americans, but also to the Brits, French, Germans, and Japanese who hand massage the cows that will become the Kobi beef that will be served at gourmet cafés in such places as Half Jaw, Lone Pine, Lame Horse, and just outside of Swan Lake, Montana, at the Bob Marshall Wilderness Dude Ranch and Spa.

All of this should only be confusing to people who take everything for granted, believe everything seen and read, and know that they are the final judge of everything making the claim to reality and truth. To such people as these—Wake up! Get over your fantasies! Denounce your delusions! This is the twenty-first century and at the Big Mountains Sky Resort Clinic just outside of Big Mountains, Montana, herds of men are getting hair replacements and tummy tucks, and women are doing Botox and undergoing breast augmentation. Boots have been replaced by running shoes, and the landscape is cluttered with life style centers, boutique farms, health clubs and condos. This is Montana, high rise and handsome.

THE NEW MONTANA
ABSOLUTELY REAL UNREALITY

Job Jr. began as a house painter. It was his father's business, and Jr., being the eldest of four, knew he would inherit it when the fumes finally put Job Sr. in the Montana State Hospital for the Psychologically Unstable. Nevertheless, this never happened because Sr. died when he fell from a twenty-foot ladder that was leaning against the windward wall of Shelby's Metal and Scrap and the wind came up. The wind can come up fast on the plains of north-central Montana, and Job Sr. should have secured his ladder, but he was in a rush that afternoon even though the completely appropriate motto of his company was "Haste Makes Waste." He landed head first in a large barrel of red paint and drowned.

One would think that that would be the end of it, but Mary Ellen, Job Sr.'s second born, was in law school at the University of Montana, and therefore knew about suing for damages. Mary Ellen contracted with a local law firm to prove that the bucket of red paint had been placed where it was because Matt Shelby, the owner of Shelby's Metal and Scrap, had not laid the flooring to city code, and hence the spot where Job Sr. was painting was too weak to support a ten gallon barrel of paint except over a joist, two-feet five-inches left of the ladder and exactly where Job Sr. would land if a wind came up. Though the defense argued that Job Sr. should have secured his ladder with rope or duct tape or something like that, the prosecution won. Whether this was a matter of Shelby' guilt, or because nobody in Shelby, Montana, liked Mayor Shelby, (the jury was composed of twelve of the thirteen adult male citizens of Shelby, Montana, a small burg on the Montana Highline founded by Matt Shelby's great great grandfather, Matthew Shelby), will never be known. The judge awarded damages of $250,000, and therefore, as Shelby's only asset was Shelby's Metal and Scrap, said business was duly transferred to Job Sr.'s offspring.

It was at this time that Job Jr. stopped painting houses, some saying he could not get past the trauma of his father's untimely death, others because he now had a fourth interest in a junkyard and the prospect of $20,000 from the sale of his father's painting business. No matter, Jr. had plans.

While on the job with his father, Jr. knew that what he scraped from peeling walls, if not eaten first by stray dogs, was simply swept up and thrown away. At the time he could only bemoan the waste, but now at the helm of JR's Metal and Scrap he thought that he might be able to do something about it. By running the paint scrapings through a cyanide leaching process that gold production companies in western Montana employed, and then fusing the residue with asbestos fibers still floating around the EPA site in Libby, he could transmute the scrapings into a product he named "acidtex" which could then be used in making everything from marital aids to faux sushi. In a word, he was in the recycled paint business; in fact, he is the inventor of that miracle fiber, "ColorFuse," the well-known commercial name of $H_2O\text{-}So_4\text{-}N\text{-}AU$ or rather, acidtex.

But this was not the end of it. While Jr. was scavenging paint scrapings from all over Montana, he surreptitiously began rounding up used computer floppies and those wafer-thin bags you get when the checkout clerk asks, "plastic or paper?," and in a rush of confusion whether to save the Brazilian rainforest or sea turtles in the south Pacific, shoppers choose the latter as saving trees allows for more of the fashionable, upscale log homes to be built in Paradise Valley. It seems that Jr.'s chief chemist and younger brother, Erik "The Red," who at the time of his trial denied ever carrying on affairs with any of several wives of Shelbians, had discovered that under low-intensity heat, or as described in the patent application, "the kind you need to get that blackened crispy coating on your marshmallow," floppies and plastic bags could be fused into radioactive lumps the size of yak droppings, and these could be sold at great profit to yurt-dwellers throughout central Asia who were desperate for synthetic yak droppings. Of course, at first people in Shelby and the neighboring towns of Browning and Flyhook laughed, but when Jr. landed a government contract for supplying the stuff, now called, "Yakattack," for a top secret Pentagon project, it was all a case of look who's laughing now.

Well, Jr.'s company became a corporation, then a conglomerate, then a multinational, reaching out to discarded beer caps, aluminum soft drink can tabs, disposed disposable Bic lighters and razors, 78, 45 and 33 rpm records, and cigarette filter tips. JR's Metal and Scrap became Job Baseline Technologies with high rise and handsome office building, stockholders, and worker morning exercise regimens. Jr. was on the cover of *Forbes* and voted 2004 Man of the Year by *High Times* magazine. The company's most brilliant move was when it contracted with thousands of Hardees, Wendys, McDonalds, and Burger Kings to buy up past-dated ketchup, mustard, and mayonnaise packets that could then be refashioned through the miracle of Red's department of Bio-Chemical

Engineering into such health club body shaping apparatus as the Bust-Builder and the Butt-Buster. Though market returns from starving third world countries and failed nation-states were nothing to talk about, they were nothing to sneeze at either.

Today, Job Highline Technologies has morphed into Job Indo-European Cell Phone Stem Cell Fuel Cells Transnational, Inc. Along the way the constant feuding between Red and Mary Ellen, the company lawyer, led to the now infamous shooting incident at the Shelby gun range. Then there was the scandalous trial which drove Job's stock value almost to nothing, and the youngest son of Job Sr., Luke Lee, who had been running the company's marital aids division, had to be let go after serving time in the same nicely decorated jail cell with Martha Stewart.

But it is funny, the twists and turns of reality. During one of his monthly visits to Luke Lee, Jr. learned that the paint Stewart used to decorate her prison cell was a particular shade of mauve that could only be made by using Indo-Flack, a pigment base on which Jr.'s company held the patent. Stewart jumped at the chance to promote Indo-Flack in prisons nationwide, and Fred's stock rebounded, better yet, soared.

Jr. is rich, admired, and just one more example of the Great Montana Success Story. He is married now to a reformed porn star who before her Hollywood career was in the final ten of the 2001 Miss America contest. And never forgetting his humble beginnings, he erected a mausoleum for his father and mother (Martha had died from over-exertion years earlier while stirring a ten gallon vat of paint for Job Sr.) that is said by many in Shelby to rival the Taj Mahal in Atlantic City. It's a lesson Iraqis, North Koreans, and others bent on nothing more than doing evil need to take to heart.

SADIE THE LADY YOU BETCHA

Even though scholars of the caliber of Aaron Hodgeson, the Velanucci sisters, and Fig Smith have claimed that Montana sheepherder Hal "Halitosis" Drinkwater invented fitted sheets, they are wrong. Hodgeson, for example, has written:

> Mr. Drinkwater, during the coldest December on record (-15 celesus) in Montana (1924), sewed the corners of a bedsheet together in an attempt to keep said sheet from sliding off his frozen and therefore slippery mattress. As crude as this action was, it created the first fitted sheet. After winter thaw, he rode his horse (Sawtooth) into Lost Track, Montana, and telegraphed the U.S. Patent Office in Washington, D.C., requesting a patent for his invention.[1]

In a follow up article the Velanucci sisters added these tantalizing details:

> Mr. Dinkwalker [sic] used white thread and a number four needle in his handiwork. The sheet was 180 count percale.[2]

As much as the world might like to credit Mr. Drinkwater with the invention of fitted sheets for both his glory and its reflection on the Montana frontier spirit, he did not invent the fitted sheet. Rather, because of a whisky spill and several smudges of what appears to be sheep dip on the patent application form, Hodgeson, et. al. misread it. Under close inspection, one conducted by employing the latest infrared technology and electron microscope magnification, it becomes clear that the patent was denied. Why denied? After more intensive research, Montana State University sociology professor Betty Goldstein discovered that a patent for fitted sheets, a second for the invention of the comforter, and a third for the pillow sham had been awarded a mere three months before Mr. Drinkwater's application to Thecla Drinkwater of Helena, Montana, who was none other than the estranged wife of Hal.

With this new information, thousands of questions began hurling through Goldstein's mind. Even if love had flown, was there still some psychic connection between the separated, by about two-thirds the state of Montana, Mr. and Mrs. Drinkwater that would drive both of them to invent fitted sheets? Then again, why did Mrs. Drinkwater think that pillows need shamming while her husband did not? Did Mrs. Drinkwater use the same size needle and the same color thread as her husband? Given that Mrs. Drinkwater sold her patents to the United Sheet and Pneumatic Brake Corporation of East Ball, New Jersey, for quite a healthy sum, could Mr. Drinkwater have demanded part of the money, having only separated from Mrs. Drinkwater and not being actually divorced?

But the most tantalizing bit of information Goldstein turned up was that Hodgeson and Smith were half brothers and that for several years Margaret Velanucci had been Hodgeson's lover before casting her lustful eye on Smith. More to the point, Hodgeson's and Smith's grandfathers on their fathers' side, were the co-directors of Research and Development at United Sheet and Pneumatic Brake Corporation in 1924!

Well, unfortunately, this is where the trail went cold which is fitting if one thinks about how cold it gets in a Montana winter. However, by going through an enormous pile of receipts at Sears and Roebuck, Goldstein learned that the first shipment of fitted sheets came up the Missouri River on a steamboat all the way from Kansas City, and was sold to one Sadie Beets (?—unfortunately, a blot of what looked to be dried KY Jelly covered the first letter, so it may be "Deets," "Peets" or "Teets") of Butte, Montana, in 1925. Goldstein wanted very badly to suppose it was "Beets," because if so, this was her great aunt on her mother's side and quite a miscreant at that.

Known to customers as "Sadie the Lady You Betcha," Sadie Beets and her girls entertained the men who came from all over southwestern Montana to her Butte bordello. Sitting high in the Rocky Mountains on a mother lode of ore that stretched far down into Mother Earth, Butte's motto was "A mile high, a mile deep, and on the level," the last phrase of which Sadie easily converted to "on the horizontal." Because innumerable single men dug in the mines of Anaconda Copper, while lonesome cowboys and forlorn sheepherders worked the surrounding ranches, Butte was littered with houses of ill repute. Sadie was the madam of the biggest and best, "You Betcha!," and if one thinks about it, her order of seventy-five sheets is entirely fitting.

NOTES:

1. Aaron Hodgeson, "The First Fitted Sheet," *Journal of Capitalist Exploitation*, Vol. 16, No. 4, 2001.
2. Margaret Velanucci and Mary Velanucci. *Why I Became . . . What Was the Question?* San Francisco: High Times Press, 2002, p. 246.

MATTHEW LUNES,
BROADWAY METEOROLOGIST

The days Matthew Lunes spent as a meteorologist at the I-90 and 27th Street underpass weather station were not as complete a waste of time as the people who did not know him but found themselves compelled to have their letters published on the Letters to the Editor page of the *Billings Gazette* have suggested. And though Lunes was totally unprepared to fulfill the specific job description of determining the effects of dew on "chip-and-seal" technology at the basement level of the 27th Street underpass, he firmly believed that he earned every dollar the taxpayers of Billings invested in the project.

Actually, Lunes was not sure how he got the job, because he had absolutely no training in meteorology. The best he can guess is when someone read the skills form he filled out at the City of Billings Employment Services Division, he or she mistook "cosmetology" for "cosmology" and thinking that the study of the complete universe was too broad, narrowed Lunes down to just weather, and then just the weather under I-90 where the expressway crosses over 27th Street.

Many people think that cosmetology is a most useful science. Practiced well, it can make good-looking people look better and people that the gods didn't provide with something worth looking at, with at least something. Endless are the virtues of heavily applied make-up to hide that motorcycle scar, the face cream to soften those facial lines carved by the winds off the Highline plains, and the wondrous variety of hair styles to cover the pieces of scalp lost during bronc busting and bull riding performances. Nevertheless, plastic surgery can only go so far in correcting a barroom brawl nose.

The time Lunes spent as a meteorologist at I-90 and 27th Street, and he knows that his tenure would have been longer if the *Billings Gazette* had not been deluged with nasty letters and three city councilmen had not been up for re-election, taught him a great deal and was a boon for the science of roadway maintenance. He learned that repeated chip applications strengthen

20

a roadbed in direct proportion to the increase in the roadbed's height. In fact, with enough layers of chip sealing, a fully loaded 18-wheeler with snow chains affixed can effect no damage to the roadbed even as the top one-third of the truck's load is sheered off while said transport maneuvers through an underpass. He also discovered that chip and seal technology makes it less likely that babies' diapers or fast food remains thrown from a moving vehicle will bounce up and splatter across the grill or windshield of SUVs or pickup trucks, though the dampening effect does little for smaller Toyotas, Fiestas, and Volkswagens.

Anyway, after Lunes moved on, he learned that his findings were being reported not only in *Scientific American* but also *House Beautiful*. Moreover, chip sealing is now being considered as a cost-effective way to floor Russia's orbiting space platform, and millions of tons of chip-seal material are being stored at military bases across the Midwest in case the U.S.'s main supplier of seals, Canada, driven by a small coterie of "Animals-Are-Humans-Too" extremists, outlaws the beating to death of the little creatures.

Matt Lunes' father always said that one day Matt would do something for humanity. Matt knows that his father now smiles down on him from heaven just as he used to coming around the 27th Street entrance ramp to I-90 on his way home to Sweet Grass.

JOHN MORRIS,
OLAMA YANDA BEN CONTADA

When his name was John Morris, he would go grocery shopping and the checkout clerk would never fail to say, "Have a nice day." The lady at the dry cleaners never failed to say, "Have a nice day." The hostesses at Applebee's, Chili's, Red Lobster, and the International House of Pancakes never failed to say, "Have a nice day." The barber and the cashier with the prison tattoo at the SuperStop gas station always greeted him with "How's it hangin'?" The kid who took tickets at the American Legion ballpark said, "How's it hangin'?" or "Hey, whassup?" And of course no one really cared how John was doin' when they asked "How you doin?" or "How's it goin'?"

Everywhere John looked there were smiley faces. They were on tickets and ticket stubs, on cash register receipts, and a law recently passed by the Montana state legislature put them on marriage and death certificates; in the case of marriage certificates, in hopes that it would stem the flood of divorces; and on death certificates, an affirming nod to, John supposed, resurrection, They were in newspaper and magazine advertisements for cars, computers, feminine hygiene products, and erectile dysfunction remedies.

Whether it took the entirety of a nice day-smiley face reality to break him or a single especially noteworthy event such as having a clerk direct a "How's it hangin'?" followed by "Have a nice day" and a receipt for $6.25 stamped with a large red smiley face for a pair of Jockey shorts imprinted with hundreds of smiley faces, might never be known, but John Morris finally broke.

A newly minted college graduate, John found a position with the Montana Bureau of Social Services after a stint as an oil and filter mechanic at Got Lubed? and then as luggage loader at the Helena Trailways bus depot. His job was to make people who had absolutely no chance of escaping their underclass status feel good about themselves. Though every file folder was stamped with a happy face, on several occasions John got into trouble with his superior when he forgot to begin an interview with "How you doin'?" and end it with a "Have a nice day." Devoted to his work, he would leave his apartment at seven a.m. so that he could get stuck in traffic on the way to the office where he could spend a good deal of time searching for a parking space which he would need to relocate at five p.m. for the traffic jamming ride back to the apartment.

Some people are better at a "Have a nice day" sort of life than others. It is not as if John didn't try, initiating a "How you doin'?" or responding with "Have a nice day" as often as he could. He liked his job at the Bureau of Social Services, his co-workers were pleasant if not especially exciting, and he was good with people who had no chance of escaping their underclass existence. He had his own cubicle where there were absolutely no restrictions on how many pictures of his family he could use to decorate.

But it was clear that something was going terribly wrong when he downloaded pictures of Condolezza Rice and Brittany Spears, tacked them up, and then told his fellow office workers that the former was his mother and the latter his estranged second wife. Things went from bad to worse when he forget to bring a grab bag present for the office Christmas party and then missed his church's New Year's Eve party for marriageable availables who could not get a date.

So no one was surprised when he joined Avanda Vey Gavartii Transformer, a New Age religion that was clearly out of touch with "Have a nice day" reality. Being Olama Yanda Ben Contada meant he could not lunch at McDonald's or Burger King anymore, but he could have all the mystical experiences that he wanted and he would not have to co-pay visits to his dentist, optometrist, or general practitioner, because he could manage his own health through a judicious blend of vitamin E, ginseng root, and ionized sesame seed juice until he got really sick. He liked a lot of the people he met in the cult after he adjusted to their body odors. They had a unique perspective on life, saying things like:

> When you come to know your mind size, then you will become crystallized spirit, and you will realize you are the son of the living Transformer. But if you refuse to know your mind size, Sri Avanda Vey Gavartii will sink you in a great pile of excrement and you will fester as living pus.

He did not understand this, but he met Huldah, a fascinating young woman who did not shave her legs or underarms and spent a lot of time naked.

Soon Olama was having wonderful mystical insights and thrilling out-of-the-body experiences. When he ordered a pizza he could say, "Make me one with everything." When he bought his naturopathic elixirs, he never took his change because he knew that change came from within. He had torrid sex with his chiropractor and anyone finished with her *après-ski* yoga workout. For one full year his neurasthenia and acne disappeared.

But like all good things, it all came to an end, for how many mystical experiences can one person handle? And Olama came to realize that his out-of-the-body experiences were getting him nowhere. Sure the Avanda Vey picnics were great, and so, too, the Monday evening Sabbath Contra Dance, but all the chanting and incense were beginning to wear on him. During meditation and suppression of heartbeat exercises, he would ask the Transformers to give him better out-of-body experiences, but he never heard back. Once, after the traditional three-day fast ending the holy season of Comka Baalah Beyu, he was granted an extraordinary vision of Reality as it will be when there will be no more "smiley faces," and though he will be eternally thankful for that, it was not enough to sustain him. He soon realized that the cult could be just as inane as the "Have a nice day" reality at the Bureau of Social Services.

Maybe Olama's out-of-body experiences were not as exciting as some people's. Capo Jovandi Lucandi, the Avanda Vey Gavartii Transformer Herbal Unit leader, caught up to him at the natural food store and simply had to tell him about her recent trip to Bali with Johnny Depp. Another Avanda Vey Gavartii Transformer member had the luck to visit the Terric Betha monastery on Saturn and took part in their May Day ritual, which Olama had heard so much about. True, he cannot deny that his *ménage à trois* with Pamela Anderson and Beyonce at a Cancun hideaway was fabulous, but everything had gone downhill since then.

And finally Olama made a terrifying discovery; millions of office workers, minor bureaucrats, store managers, and really junior executives were joining cults that advertised out-of-the-body experiences. In fact, out-of-the-body travel was becoming so popular that credit card companies began giving a mile of out-of-the-body travel for every dollar charged. One thousand mile-points got you an out-of-the-body experience to Escondido; ten thousand mile-points and you could go around the world. (This past summer American Express gave two miles for every dollar spent at the local gas station—a promotion that made absolutely no sense to anyone since you could get where you're going for free if you just waited till you were asleep. Oil stocks tanked as the gasoline glut dropped prices to twenty-nine cents a gallon.) Since Olama put all his purchases on the card, he racked up points like mad. But where to go—and, of course, though the Avanda Vey Gavartii Transformer sacred texts said that one should never feel guilty for anything, he felt guilty if he let the points go to waste.

Much of this explains why the airlines are running scared. Though people are bumping into people all night long (five to six a.m. is especially congested with a lot of people rushing to get home), there is no luggage check or lost luggage, no inedible food, and no frustration trying to get a taxi to and from the airport. True, some people at the end of their flights have found themselves in the wrong bed. Just that happened to Olama's second cousin Luke, AKA Haku Ibn Rek, when he found himself at the terminus of his flight in bed next to a blond lap dancer named Merry Quitecontraree. He had one terrible time trying to explain that flight to his wife.

So a few weeks ago around four a.m., when Olama found himself hovering above a Super Bowl Sunday promotion poster outside the Hollywood Hilton, he said "Enough of this." Why he was there he did not know; maybe he was waiting for Susie Hilton or an even more undressed Janet Jackson to show up. Olama had left his apartment at two a.m. only to get stuck in out-of-the-body traffic on the way to nowhere so he could spend a good deal of time searching for a parking space which he would need to vacate by five a.m. if he were ever to get through the traffic jamming people out of their bodies so he get back to his bed by six when the alarm rang. He was cold and bored, and he found himself wishing that someone would say, "Have a nice day," or "How's it hangin'?"

The alarm rang, and he got out of bed, took a shower, put on a tie, and decided to be John Morris again. At the office each file folder was stamped with a happy face, and John decided that he was going to work his way to the top by mastering the most convincing "How you doin' and "Have a nice day" at the Bureau. He had mastered the maze, you betcha!

DEEP QUESTIONS

The great questions are embarrassing. This peculiar fact is not made a wit less peculiar by the observation that frequently the answers suggested to these questions are even more embarrassing. One might claim that the great questions and purported answers only embarrass philosophers, theologians, and other less easily categorized intellectuals. Of course this is not the case; the unphilosophical and more easily entertained have their unrelenting quandaries, too. They ask:

- Who cleans up after a tailgate party?
- Why is there tofu and what is its relation to hamburger helper?
- Why am I here when I'd rather be anywhere else?

One can find red faces and flustered speech all the way from presidents and CEOs of anything down to the lowly bulk sewage station attendant at the local garbage dump. However, none of these questions or individuals are truly philosophical in nature.

The philosophical spend lifetimes with whether everything is reducible to matter, energy, spirit, God, or some amazingly intricate and equally obscure combination of these. They consider whether humans have a mind or body, and if both, how do they interact or is one simply an epiphenomenon (see "fart") of the other. They ponder the implications of cause and effect, force and mass, chance and probability. They need to know if it is all fate, destiny, predestination, determinism, or free will.

There must be a good reason for the existence of such embarrassing questions, even if no one has found it yet. Is it that something in human interactions with the tools of human existence demands them? Is there a metaphysical gene twisted into the double helix? Maybe they arise from an improper expression of a communal libido, or a political ideology that wreaked havoc on millions, or a great militant religion that only succeeded in producing hordes of fanatics? Could the real cause be boredom while waiting to use the single working port o'potty at the county fair?

Matthew, Mark, Luke, and John imagine one of the comely young women they saw in *Maxim*, or was it *Stuff*, standing by the bank of the Missouri River, sticking her foot into the swiftly moving waters, then taking her foot out, and then putting it again, saying, "You cannot step into the same river twice." Immediately, they begin to question why this woman would be doing this while wearing four-inch heels, black silk stockings, and a satin bandanna. Does she not have better things to do with her time like finishing that Harvard post doctoral research in comparative anatomy of which the caption to her picture speaks.

Then again Mark or Luke might ask why the woman has to be attractive. Or why she has to be young, or a woman even? Why not a man? Could she or he be a transvestite? Or maybe cross-gendered? Maybe Matthew or John should inquire into what a horse might say when the animal put its hoof in the water, that is, if it could talk. Finally, if it is impossible to step into the same river twice, is it possible to step into the same river even once?

The very bearded Swedish philosopher Hans Abscurskii once attempted to solve what has become known in the history of deep metaphysical speculation as the "Same River Quandary." He ran alongside a swiftly flowing Yellowstone River, keeping up with it as it were, and jumping in every few minutes. When Abscurkii reached the point where the Yellowstone emptied into the tumultuous waters of the Missouri, he drowned. This has raised an imponderable ethical issue for impenetrable philosophical thought: Is the proper sentiment in this case, "It serves him right"?

Various medieval theologians bothered about "How many angels can dance on the head of a pin?" and "Could God make two mountains without an intervening valley?" Various contemporary theologians still worry over a question Plato posed 2400 years ago: "Are the moral laws God revealed to humankind good because they are good, or because God said they are good?" That any of this is better than Buddhist monks who spend their days entranced by such conundrums as "What is the sound of one hand clapping" is hard to say, but who has not attempted to determine if a sound is made when that tree falls in the forest and no one is around.

"What is inside of nothing?" demonstrates an utter contempt for human rationality, and maybe that is why some people feel compelled to seek an answer to it. Humankind will not be beaten by a mere string of words ending in a question mark.

"Concentrate" it said on the side of an orange juice carton, and so Matthew, Mark, Luke, and John do. Hey, wouldn't those four-inch heels get stuck deep in the mud?

MORE IMPONDERABLES

When the Montana winter drops to zero, the worst spot to be is before the fireplace with a good Bordeaux, Oysters Rockefeller, a few slices of proscuitto, and a romantic conversation that takes a turn to the questions that plague the human soul. Of course, not everyone likes Bordeaux, so there is nothing wrong with a good Chianti or Cotes de Rhone when the five p.m. twilight slides into darkness and Mary just like John needs a bit of stimulating relaxation, and then the imponderables of everyday existence suddenly present a diabolical *coitus interruptus*. And if this isn't enough, there is always hot buttered rum, while the wind chill is pushing minus fifteen and the kids are at the neighbors or grandma's for a sleep-over, and now what must be faced has found the wrong time. Someone is being caressed, being made love to, enticed, and as small talk laces the fire-lit air, someone has to ask, "Why is there tofu?"

Ecstasy ebbs and intimacy vanishes as imponderables destroy the mood, any mood. Mary, absolutely irresistible in plunging décolleté and red patterned stockings tucked into a pair of sling-back Guccis, suddenly asks, "Why are there refried beans, chicken tenders or free range, and fake crab?" Somewhere across town, Martha is slipping off Matt's silk Armani shirt, and he suddenly cries, "What kind of civilization promotes the virtues of Jell-O, Tang, Fruit Roll-Ups, and Gator Aid?"

Soon lovemaking all over Montana turns hostile and vicious. "Can anyone really tell one bottled water from another?" "Well, of course!" "You mean, of course, not."

"Just what is the Roni in Rice-a-Roni?" "Hell, it's a lot better than Hamburger Helper."

Philosophers consider none of these questions the "Great Questions of the Contemporary Age," and of course they are wrong. Which is more important, the question of whether humans have a soul or why hamburger needs help? Most people know they have a soul, or more simply, "soul," but Mary, Mary, Mary, Martha, and Marie, Matthew, Mark, Luke, and John would bet that most people have no idea why hamburger needs help. And what kind of help? For instance:

- Does the essence of hamburger need help or just when transmuted into meat loaf or meatballs?
- Does it always need help? Picture two young people in a tender embrace suddenly falling into argument over whether hamburger eternally needs help or only on occasion, say, when it sat in the refrigerator a day too long?
- Does all hamburger everywhere need help, or just hamburger in certain locales? Picture two young people in a mid-kiss suddenly stopped by an image of a bag lady with a cardboard sign reading "anee spare chang?" and by her ill-shod feet is a plastic bag of not so freshly ground hamburger. With only a dollar to spare, these two lovers begin to argue over which should be given aid.

Mary, Mary, Mary, Martha, and Marie, Matthew, Mark, Luke, and John know that the quandaries of contemporary life can't be stopped. The fire is blazing, flaring, consuming, and suddenly a Mary asks, "If a just mixed glass of Tang is no different from fresh squeezed orange juice, are Tang and orange juice of the same substance, like substance, or is the former just substance abuse?"

John turns flaccid by this turn, but with Mary down to thong, he hopefully offers, "And if orange juice were there from the very beginning, was Tang created in time, or an offspring of orange juice but with the orange from the beginning?"

Of course, that is the destruction of what could have been a glorious evening, so it is followed by "Just how are we to understand the orange-flavored cupcake? Is it a further creation, not actually from orange juice, but derived essentially from Tang, or does it naturally proceed from both orange juice and Tang?"

These are the questions that try the human soul when better things could be at hand. It is passion destroyed as Mary and John and Martha and Matt entwine in an orgy of contemporary life's imponderables. Do the gods really want people to do this? Does not history prove that humans are better at copulation than deliberation? Why not the easy questions like when will the universe stop expanding? It so boggles the mind, you betcha.

EMPEROR JACK

After Emperor Jack's suicide attempt, the Goldsteins began paying him more attention. Had they left him at home too often? Could they have scolded him too much? Maybe, they should have been more concerned when he began urinating without lifting the toilet seat. Moses would come home from work, and instead of the usual glad greeting, Emperor Jack would cower in the pantry knowing what he had done was wrong. Was he signaling to his family that he was lonely, or depressed, or afraid that single-handed he would have to face a robber? Miriam should have caught on when she found the medicine chest open and the iodine bottle empty on the floor.

And then Emperor Jack slashed his wrists. He had climbed into the bathtub, filled it with warm water, and slashed his wrists. Moses' razor, bloodied, lay beside the tub on the floor. Dogs have paws, but do they have wrists? Whatever dogs have, there they were, all four slashed, bleeding into the warm water. It is not something anyone wants to come home to: a blood-pink broth, drooping, distraught jowls beneath downcast eyes, and a tail curled under.

But Emperor Jack had not been mistreated. He had a big yard to run in, fresh water every day, and he was never scolded when he chased the family cat. The cat never showed signs of depression. The cat slept a lot but that is what cats do. She played with a mouse filled with catnip. She had a ball that had a bell within. She had a cat bed and a sanitary litter box. Sure she demanded a lot of attention, and sure she was put out when the Goldsteins brought Emperor Jack home. Miriam and Moses could still recall how badly she behaved when they bought Red Relish.

Red Relish, a unique cross between a Panamanian parrot and a Peruvian parakeet, never joined in friendship with the cat. Even if friendship was beyond reach, the Goldsteins hoped for some sort of detente between enemies. She certainly was queen of her cage, a stunning bamboo cage lovingly crafted by the tiny hands of underfed children in India. An imported cage for an imported bird Miriam would say, they had purchased it, paying full price, at Pier 1 Imports. Red Relish had a beautiful voice, and though she refused to squawk

"Polly wants a cracker" or call out some sea captain's obscenity, the bird had mastered an aria from *Don Giovanni*. However, as the months went by the Goldsteins began noticing that the bird was singing more and more off key. As Red Relish slid downhill, they tried everything they could to save her, but Red's red was slowly turning ashen. With her feathers scattered across the base of that lovely cage, one dreary afternoon she fell naked from her bamboo perch, banged against the cuttlebone on her way down, and died.

After the suicide attempt, Moses took Emperor Jack to a psychiatrist who specialized in household pets. Dr. Steamspring had earned his reputation working with circus animals, but after his altercation with a male camel who was going through whatever constitutes a divorce in the camel world, he turned to smaller and tamer animals. The story is that the camel became enraged when Dr. Steamspring suggested that the camel's mother might be at fault in a sort of animal oedipal complex in which her offspring was unable to become fully erect unless a female dressed in his mother's saddle and bridle. The cut that crossed Dr. Steamspring's nose and ended just below his left ear had hardened into a scar that gave him a German fencing fraternity look. In fact, Dr. Steamspring would tell people that is how he got the scar. The nervous tick in his right eye could not be accounted for.

Dr. Steamspring met with Emperor Jack twice a week in fifty-minute sessions for six months. Though such sessions are confidential doctor-patient interactions, Dr. Steamspring could tell Moses that he could not find any psychological basis for Emperor Jack's depression. He administered the usual battery of tests, tried hypnosis, and did a bit of dream analysis. But though nothing showed up, Emperor Jack kept going downhill.

Whether it was luck, just plain or dumb, Miriam found the dioxin-coated hairballs that the cat had buried in its litter box. Not saying a word, she installed a small camera in the kitchen that captured the cat, when no one was looking, mixing several small dioxin-coated hairballs into the dog's food. For how long this had been going on the Goldsteins could only guess, but the cat's shocking behavior left them dazed. Where the cat got the dioxin, they didn't know, and really didn't care. They knew where the cat was getting the hairballs.

And then Scout, the Goldsteins' daughter, with tears in her eyes raised a possibility that should never have been raised. Had the cat murdered Red Relish?

ALIEN ABDUCTION

Initially, alien abduction sorely disturbed Mark and his buddies. At first they got it wrong and so kept asking each other why anyone would want to abduct an alien. Just what would you do with an Italian shoe salesman taking in the sights at Yellowstone Park? Then someone in Mark's support group got the idea that the whole thing is probably tied to the many visitations Montana has had from extra-terrestrials.

Mark carries with him the trauma that his mother never referred to him as her son, but rather "that being who's eating me out of house and home." She would say such things as "You must excuse him, he learned his manners on some other planet." A few years ago, in the "Gender and Genitalia Class" he was auditing at the local community college, he learned that men are from Mars, so now he sees that his mother was right after all, and the hostility harbored all these years against her was so much wasted psychic energy. To think, he could have been using that energy to move keys and bend spoons.

His therapist (the Montana mistress of Therapeutic Touch, Saint Helena Freebolt) has helped him recover repressed memories of the hundred and twenty-six times he was abducted and taken by inter-galactic spacecraft to Pluto, Saturn, and Cicero, Illinois. He now can recall the pain caused him when aliens using the most terrifying instruments attempted to get his shoe size. Mark daily thanks Jesus, the saints, his personal angel, and other less invasive extra-terrestrials that he was not subjected to what happened to others: those who were beaten by what passes in other galaxies for barroom brawlers or were forced to be sex slaves to Zirconium beauty queens.

Nevertheless, it remains unclear to Mark why extra-terrestrials find him more interesting than either his friends or he does. Maybe he is spending too much time moving keys, bending spoons, and standing pins on end and saltshakers on edge. He sometimes whiles away far too many hours wondering what Martians do on their day off. Sometimes it isn't Martians, but Venusians or possibly Plutonians. He asks himself, do they mutilate cattle for fun? Do they enjoy making crop circles? Why don't they just come out and say, "We are here to kill you," or "We have come in peace." And why would the U.S. government conceal such visitations—in hopes of being granted some military advantage over all the nations and states that are out to get America?—from fear of widespread panic? If rush hour on the New York subway doesn't cause a panic, why should this?

Mark stares at his friends as across their beers they stare at him, and the questioning cannot be stopped. What do Martians think as they take in the sights and tourists at Yellowstone Park or Glacier? Since Martians do not wear clothes, as Hollywood sci fi flicks have amply demonstrated (and what need is there for clothes when they hide their genitalia so well?), do they understand that people do, or do they think that shoes, pants, skirts, blouses and shirts are just another part of the human anatomy? And if extra-terrestrials were to successfully mate with essential terrestrials, would the world get a race of quintessential terrestrials or non-essential terrestrials?

Mark's mind reels. He pictures aliens trying to figure out how to work their genitalia in concert with human genitalia, so that offspring might come from the union. He imagines that female Saturnians have a penis and testicles, the latter being the bearer of unfertilized eggs. How would that work out in the back seat of his '98 Subaru? Or what if the erection of an aroused male Plutonian was constituted by a volleyball-size blister on the end of what plausibly might be his eleventh toe. Well, that might be kinky, at least.

Mark and his buddies are convinced that the cosmos is filled with aliens, and that at least some of these aliens carry intergalactic passports and devices with plugs that can be used in either 110, 220, AC or DC outlets. Mark knows that he spends too many sleepless nights on the roof of his condo waiting, just waiting, with great but anxiety-laden expectations for contact with aliens who may or may not take off his shoes in an attempt to procreate a race of quintessentials through him.

SOPHIA BEETS' GRAVITY BOOTS

Call her crazy, but Sophia Beets believes in modern science. Yes, she knows that is radical these days, what with herbal medicine, faith healing, chiropractic, bio-magnetism, therapeutic touch, ESP, channeling, Creationism, Intelligent Design, and all the other wonders of wishful thinking appealing to a curious array of neuroses and psychosomatic afflictions, but stubborn Sophia Beets still believes in science. When others at the office chant "Amateurs built the Ark . . . Scientists built the Challenger," Sophia smiles back with " . . . and just why would 'scientists' be featured in *People Magazine* if they were so misguided? Don't you at least get a notice in *Newsweek* or *Time* for thinking up a nugget like the Big Bang, or the Double Helix, or $E=MC^2$? Just try explaining why bored millionaires fly first class in an around-the-globe adventure when always-fashionable divine revelation proclaims the world to be flat, at the center of the universe, and that mere air could never support a multi-ton behemoth fancifully called and *air*-plane? At least, and to the credit of the economically challenged, when they choose coach on non-scheduled airlines they know they will be going nowhere when the plane fails to take off."

Maybe Sophia's stubbornness is genetic; did not her grandmother, Sadie Beets, black sheep that she was, insist on fitted sheets when most Montanans were still using bedrolls, horse blankets, and flat sheets?

Someone named Lampwick in Sophia's chat room typed, "All the nonsense going around about the existence of atoms would be cleared up if the government would open its X-Files on the subject." A blogger named Crystal Powers, wrote, "The Center for Disease Control is spreading disinformation about AIDS to keep Americans from traveling to third world countries and seeing the havoc consumerism is wreaking as Washington fat cats export factory jobs in order to deplete the ozone, not everywhere, but only over eco-friendly countries." Sophia did not understand this, though she guessed that to whoever wrote it, it made perfect sense.

When Sophia was thirteen she was convinced that the Bible provided incontrovertible evidence that evolution had been foisted on the un-churched

American public by a cabal of communists, secular humanists, and sexual degenerates. With God-like certainty, youth minister Caviezel, the spiritual light of Sophia's adolescent existence, warned her that if you can convince people that the cunningly crafted theories of natural selection or genetic variation are true, you could be sure that these de-souled direct descendants of apes would lose their faith, lose their moral compass, and lose their God-given sense of simple decency, and would spend the rest of their ugly lives in a stupor in some corner bar, drug den, flop house, or bordello.

And if the theory of evolution didn't do the trick there was Einstein's Theory of Relativity to mislead the unwary into believing that space and time are relative to the observer. How the passionate Caviezel tried to set Sophia straight as to what Einstein was really attempting to do, namely, convince people that everything was relative so that they would never be able to tell right from wrong, good from evil, virtue from sin, and a spiteful Satan from an all-loving, if terribly bloodied, beaten, whipped, and gored, Christ.

What all this comes down to is that some people are afraid of science and others have no idea what it actually is. Some are driven by the fear of tampering with Nature that God micromanages using breakout sessions for His minions who are only supposed to rubber-stamp what He in His divine wisdom knew from eternity he was going to do anyway. For others it is the wonders of wishful thinking, the imagined powers of cure-all elixirs, miraculous occurrences, and self-fulfilling prophecies in place of the hard and difficult work of scientific research.

Sophia drives a Subaru station wagon. It is all-wheel drive, and through winter the wheels wear studded snow tires as she drives to school board town hall church meetings in Hamilton, Hardin, Two Dot, Three Forks, and Shelby. She is introduced as Dr. Sophia Ruach Beets, here this afternoon this evening this morning to comment on the motion to outlaw the teaching of evolution, and if not that, the motion to include in the curriculum Creationism or Intelligent Design.

Sophia will say that evolution has explained the changes that species undergo. Physics has offered a measure of control over the laws of nature. Astrophysics has presented an understanding of the universe and enabled a man to walk on the moon. Subatomic physics has provided insight into the constitution of matter and offered new sources of energy. Biochemistry has clarified the structure of animal heredity and produced miracle drugs to combat and often defeat serious illnesses. Not only are these things to believe in, they are nothing less than science's great gift to humanity.

Sophia will end saying that Prometheus bringing fire to humankind has nothing on the latter-day heat generated by scoffers, the ignorant, the fearful, and the gullible. People who can quote from memory biblical scripture chapter and verse believe they can falsify any scientific theory and can produce the most amazing claims that have been fully certified by innumerable spouters of biblical scripture chapter and verse. Then there are the prophets, psychics, and purveyors of pseudo-science who have spotted ghosts, seen flying saucers, and had brain tumors removed along with sizable portions of their frontal lobes.

Sophia Beets, Ph.D., member in good standing of the American Academy of Sciences and the National Science Foundation, understands that to be anti-science is to be fashionable. How paradoxical that these post-modern throwbacks to Medieval darkness are multi-tasking at their cell phones and computers as they check their palm pilots while preparing their micro-waved deep-frozen and irradiated dinners. And Dr. Beets takes pleasure in knowing that her female auditors are stuffed into the well-researched cantilever dynamics of push-up bras intended to drive her Middle Ages male auditors to reach for the great trinity of modern chemistry, Rogaine, Lipitor, and Viagra.

SEARCHING FOR GOD IN MONTANA

If Montana is in the midst of a culture war, which it is, and Montana culture is fundamentally Christian, which a lot of people want to believe is the case, then the only peace that can be expected is when Montana's two Christianities can find a peaceful resolution of hostilities. Maybe if lifelong devotees, new converts, and those who have been born again or again and again could agree on whether or not to put Christ back into Christmas, get prayer back into the classroom, post the Ten Commandments on courtroom walls, build crèches on the lawns of city government buildings, and date God's creation of the world at 4004 B.C., then surely the divorce rate will drop to zero, crack-labs will go out of business, pornography will disappear from the internet, poverty will be vanquished, and the lions of war will lie down with the lambs of peace.

The first several hundred years of Christianity were several hundred years of innumerable faiths vying to be orthodox Christianity. Bishops, elders, priests, monks, and simple peasants fought over who were to be the Real Christians and who were to be the less-than-real Christians, or the God-forsaken God-damned heretics, apostates, unrepentant pagans, Satan—worshipping barbarians, and demonic heathens. However, our epoch, the epoch of the Christian faithful, possesses this distinctive feature: it has simplified religious antagonisms. Continuing to paraphrase Karl Marx, the only difference between the first centuries of Christianity and today is that today Christianity as a whole is more and more splitting up into two great hostile camps, into two great religions directly facing each other—"Christians" and "Real Christians." The Christians can be identified by their revulsion at *The Passion of the Christ*, while the Real Christians can be identified by their tears flooding the lobbies and halls of movie theatres across Montana. Of course, this may be wrong and orthodoxy will be determined by who floodest the most—a holier than thou approach to spirituality.

Far ahead of other Americans, Montanans have come to understand that there are two Christian denominations. Away with Roman Catholics; Greek, Syrian, and Russian Orthodox; Episcopalians; Northern Baptists and Southern; Lutherans, Wisconsin or Missouri; Fundamentalists, Neo-Evangelicals, and Pentecostals. One denomination of Christianity is ecumenical, social gospel, full of love, and maybe just more than a tinge humanist and secular. The second denomination is Christianity triumphant—a personal salvation-centered faith, and hell-fire and brimstone militant. The former attempts, often too simply, a live and let live philosophy while the latter promotes, often too stridently, the One and Only Truth, whether or not the promoter has any knowledge of it. That both groups are patriotic, and therefore want government out of their lives but not out of other people's bedrooms, goes without saying.

Must innocent bystanders suppose that one of these two Christianities will inherit the Earth or at least Montana? Must they worry over what the God of the Christians has planned for Montana's un-saved Jews, Moslems, Hindus, Buddhists, Confucians, New Agers, Zoroastrians, Bahá'ís, Rastafarians, and Secular Humanists? If history is any guide, some will be lost and others will be forcibly converted. A few of the lucky ones will hide out from the pogroms in the mountains of western Montana until the frenzy passes.

SAINT HELENA FREBOLT, PSYCHIC HEALER

For ten years Dr. Lukas Smyth-Janes, Chief of Psychic Surgery at the Missoula Hospital for the Incurably Inane, had lived in fear of the Director of Psychic Nursing, Saint Helena Frebolt, whose specialty was a certain laying on of hands known to professionals as Therapeutic Touch. The investigating committee noted that the more successful she was, the more fearful he became both of the control she seemed to exercise over him and being put out of business. It wasn't always like that for when she first joined his team he fell madly in love with her after a single application of therapeutic manipulation had solved an erectile dysfunction that even Viagra couldn't touch. The next morning being Easter, Frebolt, speaking in tongues, announced, "Penus erectilus mibaba." Later she would add, "He has risen!" to her office stationery.

With his fear steadily growing and the Director of Psychic Nursing's fame spreading, Smyth-Janes fled Incurably Inane and under the assumed name of Luke S. Smith-Jones, hid out as the emergency room psychic surgeon at the Three Forks Community Clinic in Three Forks. Frebolt became a Pentecostal Cabalist master and a black belt Qi Qong therapist.

To understand this series of events one must go back to a presentation Smyth-Janes made to the International Assembly of Alternative Healing and Herbalists in 1993. It seems that somewhere toward the end of an otherwise brilliant talk, he committed a tremendous howler by announcing that TM stood for Trade Mark. All those who well knew that TM stood for Transcendental Meditation immediately sent flying toward Smyth-Janes dead rodents from psychology department experiments gone awry, and all he could do was cower behind the lectern. In the next issue of the Psychic Phenomenon Association's journal, *Real Disturbing Stuff*, his error was stamped "Gaff of the Year"[1] by the editors.

Of course, it was this embarrassing event that undermined Smyth-Janes' sexual performance. His third wife, whom everyone knew as a devoted and lovely and supportive woman, filed for divorce. The divorce was followed by a near death experience when a naturopathic healer put Smyth-Janes on a tofu and toffee diet to cure his erectile problems and the balding at temples and crown.

It was shortly after this last unfortunate event (Smyth-Janes saw no one waiting for him at the end of the tunnel) that Saint Helena Frebolt was appointed Director of Psychic Nursing at Incurably Inane. Learning of the TM gaff, his divorce, his near death experience, and his sexual shortcomings, Frebolt thought she might be able to help. Opening her red negligee psychic nursing uniform to reveal a red bustier with garters attached to silk stockings that ran just a few inches short of her thong and wearing four inch heels, she began her touch therapy. Miraculously, Smyth-Janes' inability to use his penis for anything other than urinating was corrected within minutes.

Internationally acclaimed therapist Prof. Henry Crunchk (Capt., Royal Grenadiers) has assured humankind that it is okay to enjoy one's fetishes, and Dr. Smyth-Janes spent hundreds of hours with Freebolt learning that lesson. As Crunchk noted in *Behavior and Other Things People Do*, "Pleasuring is best understood as the pro-active ingestion of the bipolar energy flow of cosmic regurgitation by integral reduction and visceral expansion."[2] But as news of Frebolt's success with Smyth-Janes spread, Smyth-Janes became fearful of the control that Frebolt exercised over him and of losing patients to her obvious therapeutic abilities. Turning to irrational acts, he began spending Sunday mornings at a local motel with young women of disrepute whom he would outfit in bustiers, push-up bras, corsets, French cut panties, thongs, stockings with and without patterns, and shoes and boots of various heights, desperately attempting to escape Saint Helena Frebolt's magical hold on him. While Frebolt was deep in prayer at the Pentecostal Holiness Fen Shiu Church of Christ, Smyth-Janes was deep into anyone who had the right costume.

But nothing worked and so he ran to his Three Forks hiding place where he was recently discovered last December through a Google search Frebolt conducted for an old high school sweetheart, whose name as best she could remember was Loomis Smith or Louie S. Jones or something like that. She typed in a variety of similar names, and when "Luke S. Smith-Jones" seemed right, she emailed. Though certainly not Frebolt's high school romance, Dr. Smyth-Janes alias Luke S. Smith-Jones knew his days were numbered for as soon as the spring melt came to the Montana Highline, the roads would be cleared and he was sure Frebolt would come after him. Gripped with paranoia, he knew she would be his death, though he and the women he would costume could not explain why.

Daily he watched the snow melt and waited for Frebolt's Hummer. Fear and trembling gripped his soul as he spent his sleepless nights reading Kierkegaard and watching Woody Allen movies. It all became too much, and in the suicide note, he wrote, "Fear of the unknown is really no worse than the fear of the known, especially if it is Friday night and one's choice is between the certainty of no date and a blind date." He obviously could not bring himself to believe it. Frebolt found him hanging from the showerhead by a Victoria's Secret garter belt. Her brother Saint Paul cut him down.

NOTES:

1. "Editorial Comments," *Real Disturbing Stuff*, vol. 18, no. 3, Fall 1993.
2. Crunchk, Henry. *Behavior and Other Things People Do*. Battle Creek, MI: Cerial Publishing Co., 1989.

C.D. LUKOVICH,
SIZE MEANS NOTHING

Because the thought is too disturbing, C.D. Lukovich, son of Anne and D.C. Lukovich of Lukovich's Television and Appliance Store, refuses to believe that last December 25, while Santa was delivering toys, the entire cosmos and all its contents doubled in size. After D.C. was put out of business, C.D. became manager of Wal-Mart's electronics aisle, where on a snow-covered December 26 morning he was informed by Marie Golly, manager of the K-Mart plus-size brassiere and panty aisle, that everything got twice as big and as heavy as everything was the day before—even time had expanded with each minute fatted by sixty expanded seconds. Maybe, because C.D. is in love, he lets a lot of things pass.

C.D. loves Marie, her smile, her petite frame, her quaint brilliance. She has a Ph.D. in mining technology from Montana Tech School of Mines, but with the shutting down of the Berkeley Pit, she found her future at K-Mart. Why she found it necessary on that snow-covered morning to leave K-Mart and drive to Wal-Mart to tell C.D. about the doubling mystified C.D. Why someone her size was the manager of the 44E and up brassiere and matching panty aisle mystified both Marie and him. But he had fallen in love, and so C.D. let a lot of things pass.

C.D., like many others, has great difficulty with such twice-as-large disturbing thoughts. He fumbles when confronted by them, and so he goes to the King's Table or a Golden Trough buffet and consumes everything. It is like being told that when God created the world in 4004 B.C., He made it look as though it had been around for millions of years, petrifying dinosaur bones and burying vast pools of oil just to test people and to separate the 144,000 true believers from the rest. So on that snow-covered morning, the day of the long return-gift lines at the customer satisfaction counters at stores all over Montana, Marie assured him that there is nothing strange about this cosmological doubling; in fact, it has been going on since the mid-seventeenth century, around the time Bishop Ussher determined after a thorough study of the Bible that the world was created just 6000 years ago.

When faced with the imponderables of life, and unable to eat anything more or enjoy sex, C.D. would go to church resale shops and purchase little things hoping against hope that they would serve as protective totems against unsettling thoughts. He would buy statuettes of Joseph or Mary, polypropylene area rugs featuring the Annunciation, and refrigerator door accoutrement with Jesus in glory and blue glitter and "Jesus Saves" in red glitter just below. And if C.D. could not get to a church resale shop, he would open a catalogue and dial up the eight hundred number or go online, whatever it took, to pursue a plastic salt and pepper shaker duo shaped as Peter and Paul or a three wise men pen, pencil, and marker set. Being in love, Marie let a lot of things pass.

Plastics have made America what it is today—the world leader in cultural innovation. Take away plastic imitations of cotton, wood, rubber, and steel, and what would America be?—a starving third world country totally unable to build adequate sewer systems or stockpile nuclear weapons. Take away plastic and no more Wal-Mart, Shopko, Target, or J.C. Penney. Take away plastic and no more front grill like the one on Marie's Subaru that was crushed as the car slid across the K-Mart parking lot ice on her return from C.D. No more mock mistletoe, holly, or Christmas trees and two-thirds of the presents beneath. American civilization is only a plastic credit card away from barbarism.

Yet, if the truth were known, plastics have done little to advance the America intellectual enterprise. "No child left behind" is the slogan, but what is she or he supposed to get even with or in front of? So, maybe the world was created 6000 years ago and made to look millions of years older, and just maybe it really does grow bigger and bigger each night or at least last December 25 without anyone knowing.

In the 17th century the world was only as big as the opposable thumb, but since people, including Queen Elizabeth and Shakespeare, giants in their own time, were only the size of an atom, no one noticed. Today, the cosmos is as big as, well, it is, but since everyone is proportionately larger, no one really notices it, except maybe a few of C.D.'s relatives for whom he really does not care, anyway. And C.D. Lukovich does not think that it has anything to do with the fact they live in double-wides (which used to be only single-wides) and that they never fail to super-size their food at McDonald's and Burger King. As for Marie and C.D., since they are in love, they let a lot of things pass.

BRONCS, BULLS, AND MEN

In the summer there are a lot of rodeos in Montana. Some people do not find them boring.

MARY ELLEN SWENSON, RASTAFARIAN

Mary Ellen Swenson never became a Rastafarian. Maybe it is because she does not hang at Starbucks or carryout tofu places and other spots Rastafarians are known to congregate. Maybe it is because they wear dreadlocks; a knit green, red, and black cap; dirty clothes; and smoke ganjah; and Mary Ellen has to wear a suit and white blouse at Job Indo-European Cell Phone Stem Cell Fuel Cells Transnational, Inc. Maybe, it all comes down to whenever her sister-in-law and Montana's ex-Lutheran neo-Evangelical Rastafari minister, Satai Olafson, asks her to become a Rastafarian she doesn't come off as really caring what Mary Ellen is, does, or believes. However, intoned to a reggae rhythm, "I care, yes I do, I really do de do de do," is the Rastafarian creed.

Such is not the case with Real Christians. Real Christians, with the greatest display of sincerity humanly possible, ask the non-saved to convert to Real Christianity, constantly. Maybe if Real Christians smoked ganjah this would not happen, or at least not happen so frequently, but Real Christians do not smoke ganjah or frequent Starbucks. Real Christians are always ready to convert anyone at any time at any place (excepting Starbuck's). If Montana is in the midst of a culture war, it is one in which Real Christians get in fights with people they call Not-So-Real Christians or Less-Than-Real Christians, or The Heretics, because the so-called Less-Than-Real Christians claim that they are the Real Christians and the Real Christians (the party of the first part) are not for real at all, at least not as real as the Real Christians (the party of the second part). Maybe it all comes down to which Real Christians have been born again more times than the Not-So-Real Real Christians.

As Real Christianity got started by a Jew named Paul who said people must walk in the footsteps of a Jew named Jesus and his Jewish apostles, Rastafarianism got started by Rastus Farina who might be the most recent apostle of a divine transcendence to grace the less-than-divine with his presence and to lead humanity toward the light and heal the lame and succor the depressed, but not pay off any credit card debt. As the gospel goes he passed his short life on a Caribbean island cutting sugar cane, sharing his wisdom with those who were stupid, and turning acid rain to Acid (a wondrous mystical drug). In the background somewhere Bob Marley is singing and Haile Selassie, past emperor of Ethiopia and present Rastafarian living god, is enthroned.

Farina could not have been an apostle of the divine unless he was ridiculed by free thinkers as a stage-show magician, by seekers of the truth as a false messiah, as the running dog of capitalists by a local cabal of communists, or by Real Christians as some New Age fake. Arrested on trumped up parking violation charges, he was force-fed cheeseburgers and French fries which killed him until a huddle of wailing female disciples saw him waft from his grave skyward on a great cloud of ganjah smoke.

So there is Mary Ellen Swenson standing at the Butte airport waiting for what seems an eternity while her bags are searched for guns, knives, and sanitary napkins stuffed with explosives, and her fingernail file is taken from her. Or she is trying to hail a cab in Billings for what seems like an eternity. Or she is in line at Wal-Mart and someone with a tremendous amount of matted, long stringy hair shoves a two-page pamphlet into her hand while whispering into her ear something about the eternal bliss in heaven that could immediately be Mary Ellen's if she would only die now.

Mary Ellen may want to know more about this heaven that she should die for, but as Satai Olafson disappears in a cloud of ganjah smoke, her place is magically taken by a Real Christian who she knows must be, because he is pasted with bumper stickers reading "In case of the Rapture, this car will be unmanned," and "Jesus died to make television evangelists rich." So there is Mary Ellen, waiting for an eternity in the airport terminal, waiting for a cab, waiting to pay for groceries, and everyone who is anyone wants to save her soul, send her to heaven, and heal where Dr. Scholls has failed.

Their search for God completed, too many people who have found salvation feel compelled to remake others in their own image. However, at the risk of losing her eternal soul, Mary Ellen would rather that her savior, Rastafarian or other, pay off her credit card debt, or at least find her a cab on a wintry night.

GETTING RIGHT WITH GOD

Not long ago a kind little voice on Hosanna Wright's answering machine announced that God loved her, and that the voice was praying for her salvation. Life is not easy, so it is nice to pick up the telephone and every so often get greeted by a cheery message.

Unfortunately, the voice did not stop there. Hosanna next learned that if she failed to "Get right with God," she was destined for the eternal tortures of Hell. She would be thrown over and over again into a fiery pit to burn eternally, the carcasses of rotting rats would be stuffed down her throat eternally, and her flesh will be flailed raw and really bloody by Mel Gibson. She had not heard of the rat-stuffing before, so she thought that the voice might be making things up as it went along. Nevertheless, originality has its virtues.

TV evangelists serially assure their legions of devotees that not only does God so love the world that he had his son murdered, but He especially loves those living sinful, wicked, immoral, corrupt, debauched, and depraved lives, and He is ready if such as these will just say the Word, to reach out and save them one and all. Hosanna is a bit disconcerted by the depth of compassion for her evil existence these loving purveyors of God's love can display. Have they been watching her? Did they overhear her when she used foul language last December when her snowmobile died in the middle of Yellowstone Park? Do they go through the discarded mail in her garbage can? The pastor and CEO of a Billings industrial size church operation once told Hosanna's father that God loves his daughter, but if she does not accept Christ as her personal savior she will go to Hell possibly tomorrow when God hurls a great meteor toward Earth to put an end to life as humans know it. If not a meteor, He might send a cosmic whale to swallow the Earth, or a disease even worse than God's shot across the bow, AIDS. How unsettling it all is.

In Montana "Get Right With God" has taken on a whole new meaning. I t used to be something about rejecting the Satanic life of the libertine. This meant things like "A family that prays together stays together," which was church on Sunday morning. It meant not branding someone else's cattle, and limiting one's carousing to Saturday night. Now it means voting against satanic liberalism. As Dr. Dobson of Focus on the Family fame has divined, it did not say in the original, "Satan get thee behind me," but "Satan get thee to the Left of me."

Have one and all been convinced that liberals are effete snobs and the nattering nabobs of negativism? Liberals are also atheists. They scoff at Jerry Falwell and Pat Robertson. They do not heed the sage advice of Rush Limbaugh. They switch channels when Fox news comes on. They read the *New York Times* and the *Atlantic Monthly*. They support gay marriage, stem cell research, and women's rights. They have been duped into believing that evolution is how humans got here and the Big Bang is how it all began. They think you are your brother's keeper, not understanding that when Cain answered God with "Am I my brother's keeper?" God thundered, "Of course you're not. If Abel would get off his food stamp aid to dependent children welfare duff, he could be just as successful as any televangelist."

But Hosanna gave up being an effete snob and the nattering nabob of negativism years ago, so why she got the phone call, she does not know. Maybe the call came from a century when they burned people at the stake; maybe it came directly from God or from someone posing as Him. Yes, of course, Hosanna should know; she is a philosophy professor, and she deals with questions like that from eighteen year olds who have the Truth. Besides, she is at a Catholic college, and like other professors at such institutions of divine revelation, they are the first to learn of a newly discovered Eternal Truth, because they read the latest encyclicals from the pope who being the Supreme Being's vicar on Earth does not have to wait in line to talk with Him. For instance, she knows the Church's stand on child sexual abuse which is that God doesn't want unmarried girls of fourteen to have sex and that is why God sexlessly inseminated Mary.

American fundamentalists, the Pentecostals and neo-Evangelicals, however, know that the pope is really the anti-Christ, and only Real Christians have access to what God is thinking every second. What God thinks is that everyone should vote Republican because Jesus was the founder of the Republican Party. Because God is white, there was a time when He demanded that everyone vote for politicians who would keep "neegras" in their place, but He has since changed his mind about the ones who are Republicans.

A growing presence in Montana is Islam, and since each and every Muslim has direct access to God, each and every Muslim knows that Allah is no trinity and therefore could not have been a Christian. Allah has no need of a Holy Spirit, especially one in the form of a pigeon, and He does not inseminate fourteen-year old girls even if it is okay for Muslim men to do this. Since Mohammad was a social conservative, meaning no strong drink and wives are to be respected and beaten, he voted Republican. But since the Republicans support the State of Israel, he voted for the Democrats. Mohammad can do that because God allowed him to perform miracles.

Jews, of course, years ago were denied direct or any other kind of access to God, because they murdered Jesus, and they do not believe that Mohammad is Allah's prophet. That the Jews did not know that they were killing God's son makes no difference, and that Jesus, Mary and Joseph and the apostles were Jews, not Christians makes no difference. Before the State of Israel came into existence and the invention of the Palestinian, Moslems liked Jews, most of the time, and only beat them when like women, they needed it.

The Hebrew Scriptures, the Christian Bible, Islam's Koran, possibly even the Baghavad Gita and the Upanashads are sacred and inerrant texts, the very words of God, and for millennia they have served devotees as an excuse for all the wrongs they enjoy committing. It is all so confusing, so unsettling, and all Hosanna wants is to confirm her suspicion about why someone is breathing hellfire and damnation into her answering machine. It is so confusing that sometimes her unredeemed self wants to go back to the womb, anyone's, though preferably a good-looking blond's. Maybe all she needs is an attitude adjustment or the *Avanda Vey Gavartii Transformer Handbook of Truth and Wisdom* so she too can get far right with God.

She would really like to.

You betcha!

JOE TUNSDALE, LIFE IN A JEWEL CASE, OR POSSIBLY A NUTSHELL

On January 1, 2004, Joe Tunsdale turned eighty and his wife Mary Sue Louise summed up his life with her gift, the four-volume CD set, "The Collected Works of Spike Jones." Neither Joe nor Mary Sue Louise nor four children all grown with children of their own were thinking of the films of Spike Lee or Spike Jonez, but rather the outlandish composer of unrefined and indefinable nonsense, Spike Jones, orchestra leader nonpareil from 1940 to '60. Joe has no doubt that his wife of fifty years knows him well, but to have one's life packaged and shrink-wrapped by the four-volume "The Collected Works of Spike Jones" captures more of one's existence than can easily be faced and certainly not want exposed to even the smallest circle of family and friends.

During December Mary Sue Louise received ten Victoria's Secret catalogs, no fewer and more than two a week, displaying such necessities as lace and latex push-up under-wire cleavage-enhancing 1958 Cadillac bumper protrusions set over matching panties that almost fail to exist. Joe does not think these catalogs say anything about Mary who must have got in on the Victoria's Secret mailing barrage when she bought a belt from that institution of exceptionally tall and weightless females in1981.

But Mary Sue Louise is able to sum up Joe's life with "The Collected Works of Spike Jones"—his entire life from birth to eighty—his unsatisfactory performance in the second grade, his Carroll College valedictorian speech, his stint as a Second World War non-commissioned government issue, first job, second job, attorney at law in Billings, and getting to third base with Sharon Reedhorn finally. Then there was first and only wife, Mary Sue Louise Souterlan, children, house, travels, three dogs, two cats, and a hamster that showed no affection for Joe. There were Saturday nights with a barbershop quartet or a polka band, and Sundays in the choir of Our Lady of the Valley Catholic Church.

Does the meaning of life, Joe's life at least, really come down to such songs as "Horsey Keep Your Tail Up," "Barstool Cowboy from Old Barstow," "When Yuba Plays the Rhumba on the Tuba," and "I'm Forever Blowing Bubble Gum"? Is he not a constitution of body and God-seeded soul, but rather a bizarre collection of popguns, klaxons, car horns, washboards, doorbells, cowbells, rubber razzers, and an assortment of pots and pans from B flat to C sharp? Certainly that is the raison d'etre of "Spike Jones and his City Slickers," but of Joe Tunsdale?

Here is a life as a series of lyrics, a musical collage of "put the cat out—I didn't know it's on fire," "people are funnier than anybody," "all I want for Christmas is my two front teeth," "don't hit grandma with a shovel," and "leave the dishes in the sink, ma'."

The truth is that though Joe had aspired to the heights of Tom Lehrer, musical satirist and Harvard math professor, his wife and the ten or twelve people Joe had been fortunate not to have alienated somewhere along the way know his life as a series of pratfalls to the depths of a Spike Jones. Joe would even be satisfied for his life-record to read, "He succeeded in reaching the greatness of John Puleo and the Harmonicats" (favorites of the Ed Sullivan Show audience until upended by the clever hands of Señor Wences), but he guesses that is not to be. So after blowing out the candles he sings,

"The polar bear sleeps in his little bear skin, He sleeps very well I am told, Last night I slept in my little bare skin, and I got a heck of cold." and thanks to Spike Jones, the Boys in the Backroom, and the City Slickers for framing his life.

GODDESS WATER HEATER

After leaving his teaching post, Red Fishburn made his living serving people who enjoy what is called "white water rafting." A group of say eight or ten foolhardy souls would climb into one of his oversized rubber rafts and brave a fast flowing Montana river filled with jagged rocks and falls to be scared silly and have fun. Since people have been known to die having this fun, Fishburn's insurance premiums were only slightly less than an obstetrician's.

Some people relish breaking through four inches of lake-covering ice and then in skimpy bathing suits plunging through said break to approximate swimming for a second or two. This is also called fun, and if there are enough people about who know how to use such safety equipment as a reach pole, knotted rope, hot tea or coffee, and thermal blankets, the ice-water jumpers have been known not only to survive the plunge but also to carry on in the same way next year.

A *National Geographic* kind of fellow, Fishburn considered these sorts of undertakings to be American adaptations of the Indian fakir tradition of tiptoeing through long beds of fiery hot coals. Even better comparisons might be Sufi *zikr* practices or Yakuza finger amputation. However, he did not think that such activities are considered fun.

Yet none of these can compare to, nor should be brought up in the same breath, sentence, paragraph, monograph, book, or weighty tome, as the truly outrageous, the truly devil-may-care sport of the truly life-risking homosapien. What Fishburn was thinking about is the hyper-xtreme sport of the modern woman and man who leave prudence to the wise and sanity to the sane, and submit their hardened bodies and well-tempered souls to a six a.m. shower in water that the All Powerful All Omnipotent Divinity of Hot Water refuses to heat. Hell's minions know no punishment equal to the *danse macabre* of a bed-blanket warm body withering from shocks of sharpened shards of an ice-water shower.

She stands, Great Goddess Hot Water Heater, hidden from view, seeded in a basement Hades, and in a vicious swipe at humankind, She refuses to warm up to the dirty, sticky, oily, or sweaty. In command of time, space, and simple creaturely comforts, today She heats, but tomorrow morning She freezes. Lost in some diabolic revelry, She challenges those foolish enough to think they can tempt fate with their more than xtreme sport of risking life, limb, and soul by tempting the Great Goddess Hot Water Heater at six a.m.

Does She laugh as human flesh shrivels and the human body convulses in a thousand attempts to defy the ice water shower? Does She revel in the shock She will give those who forget the fragility of fat and muscle? Does She ignore the mantra of the Coldwater Sport enthusiasts, "Grant, oh Great Mistress, H2O at 110°"? "Of course, my dears," She howls at foolhardy humans who dare the Coldwater Sport nonpareil.

And so for all the Matthews, Marks, Lukes, and Johns, who are not weak of heart, for all those Marys, Marthas, and Maries, who strain for the next xtreme sport, welcome to Red Fishburn's "Greatest Challenge on Earth." Welcome to a frigid winter morning in Fishburn franchised shower stalls at guest homes, hostels, and hotels scattered throughout the mountain towns and ski slopes of Western Montana. Welcome to the Coldwater Sport center bar none. Prepare as one will: spend hours at the local health club or Olympic training fields; harden the body; ready the psyche; jettison woolen blankets, the warm, furry robe, the wrapping towel, and soap-on-a-rope. Fishburn and the Great Goddess Hot Water Heater cater to people who play with their lives as if there was no tomorrow.

INDIANS

There are a lot of Indians in Montana. Some people say that the Indians have been treated poorly and could use help. Others say that the Indians in Montana are rapidly being replaced by the Republican Party. Still others want to give Indians back their native land, India.

NEWS GALORE

It is no one's fault but Adam's that he lost his job. If Adam had read the newspaper once in awhile, or at least the sports pages, or tuned in on the five o'clock news, this would not have happened. Adam Golly stands silently by when his boss begins talking about those Boston Patriots Miami Dolphins Green Bay Packers Seattle Seahawks Detroit Pistons.

Adam's eldest daughter, Marie, crashed her Subaru in the K-Mart parking lot last winter, and he refuses to hear about it. Though Adam's wife has told him of the affair she carried on for two years with her sister's husband after Adam's quadruple bypass surgery, unfazed Adam still invited everyone to the Fourth of July Golly campout at the usual spot in the Bob Marshall wilderness. When a devastating windstorm blew through Helena in September, he was quietly trimming his tomato plants at his uncle's ranchette out in Clancy. If Adam knows that his long time lover, Ellie Steamspring, committed suicide by smashing into the wall at Peterson's bakery, he isn't saying.

With a B.A. in political science from Rocky Mountain College, Adam Evelyn Golly was elected state representative from his district after making a name for himself at the local Wal-Mart greeting customers and occasionally rounding up shopping carts. He then parlayed his lack of knowledge of economics into a managerial position with the State of Montana Revenue Department. Adam's great achievement was to simplify a certain regulation in the tax code which before he re-worked it had decreased everyone's taxes unless they earned more than $10,000 per annum after such exclusions as dental costs for dependent children under two or over twenty-seven and three quarters, or they were still making payments on cars purchased new but not from dealers, if and only if the family residence was a house of less than 1225 square feet and the yard was fenced.

Sitting with Adam at the Rusty Stirrup Grill last month, his co-workers realized that he had no idea whether post modernism still reigns unchallenged or has died a well-deserved death. He can only guess that political correctness has finally succeeded in transforming Orientalist scholars into Islamicists. He says that since he does not live in a center of news-fabrication such as New York or Washington, events of greatest importance do not reach him until said events have been completely surpassed by other news of greatest importance. Co-workers were amazed that he had nothing to say about the widely advertised benefits of aromatherapy, that he thinks that people now pray in rap, speaking in tongues is channeling, and that meth refers to mentholated throat lozenges. Apologetically, he says that since he does not live in a center for culture-fabrication such as Los Angeles or Taos, the news of discoveries of the greatest importance do not reach him until the discovery has been discovered to be without merit.

Adam's computer-driven friends who work at the Mansfield Revenue Building but who live in cyberspace have told him that the Internet would solve his problem, which they then informed him does not exist anymore because now there are only issues. They told him that by having CBS, or NBC, or ABC, or the *New York Times* online as his home page, the world would be at his fingertips. So, in the interest of making his office buddies happy, Adam turned to the Internet, but all he got were viruses, worms, and email spam that insulted the size of his penis, exaggerated the amount of his hair loss, and would he like to have torrid sex with a midget. So he installed a spam-blocker, Norton anti-virus, Symantec updates, Adware and Spybot, and now it takes his computer so long to download what looks like an interesting item that he might bring to the coffee room or water fountain that by the time he gets it, everyone else has moved on to the latest Boston Patriots Miami Dolphins Green Bay Packers Seattle Seahawks Detroit Pistons scores.

What it really comes down to is that though this is 2005 in an up-to-date Montana, high rise and handsome, Adam has chosen to live in a 1950s television sitcom. He still shops at J.C. Penney's, Sears, and the local five and ten that he recognizes in the new One Dollar Store that sells kitsch to his teenager daughter. Adam's house, as difficult as it is to believe, is in an actual neighborhood. He knows the people who live next door. They have a dog named Sally and a cat named Sam and some sort of bird. Martha, his wife, can run across the street without looking both ways for cars on their way to a drive-by shooting and ask Anita Klown, another 50s holdover, for a cup of sugar. In the summer Last Chance Gulch, main street, is closed on Wednesday evenings for street dances. The only discordant note to Adam's Eisenhower Years is a drug-pushing operation known as DARE in his daughter's high school.

In his co-workers' attempt to keep up with Adam's take on current events, they once listed all the news he has gotten wrong during the years they have known him.

- Princess Diana died in a horrific boating accident on the River Seine. Adam thought that she had just left a fundraiser at the Paris Ritz for children with sickly polo ponies, when her speed boat, piloted by the love of her life, Prince Charles, struck a dynamite-jacketed Palestinian suicide bomber in a rubber raft on his way to Friday night Sabbath services at a local synagogue. People the world over are demanding sainthood—some want it for Diana, others for the Palestinian.

- In a strange twist of fate when the Pope visited Israel he convinced Ariel Sharon to become Catholic while the Pope in a show of Christian love converted to Judaism.
- Pakistan and India went to war with each other over the issue of which country is more peace-loving. As nuclear weapons exploded, the Prime Minister of India announced that in a spirit of respect and compassion he would keep killing Muslims until they realized that Hindus treated people of all faiths better than Muslims did.
- A small cabal of Jewish bankers once again is running the world. They are also behind global warming.

Was Adam's job at the Revenue Department worth knowing about what is going on in the world? Should his friends have helped him? Bring him up to date? Then, they remembered the one event he got right and when they saw the tears in his eyes they thought that maybe he was better off than the rest of them. He knew far too much about the horror of 9/11.

So Adam lost his Revenue Department job. It seems that he was passing out homemade cookies to trick or treaters, and a mother threatened to sue the State of Montana when she saw that the treat was not a store-bought, pre-wrapped candy and Adam could have put pins in the cookies to kill all the children who came by. If only Adam had read the news that millions of children all over America were dying from pins, glass shards, and razor blades hidden by evil people in homemade goodies, who doubts that he would have run over to the One Dollar Store and bought bags of pre-wrapped airport-scanner-ed candy.

It is no fault but Adam's that he lost his job. Of course, he did not know he lost it until he came to work on Monday morning and his cubicle had disappeared.

WHERE HAVE ALL THE BUFFALO GONE?

While lunching at the local J.B. Big Boy's, Mary Larkin knocked her car keys off the table just after getting into a pretty good twice-baked potato stuffed with sour cream, chives, and synthetic bacon bits. Her keys fell and though they fell toward the floor, they never got there. Somewhere between the table and the floor the keys slipped from their descent and disappeared. Mary knows that they did not reach the floor because a thorough search conducted not only by her but also by a waitress and two busboys failed to locate them. True, the waitress was too fat to do much good as she was unable to crawl under the table, but the busboys who looked as if they were members of their high school's long-distance running team scoured the under-table cavern and turned up nothing. At the next table the Shelton brothers joked that a mouse must have carried them off until the manager came over and announced that Big Boys do not have mice and if the Sheltons mentioned to anyone either that things disappear at her restaurant or that same is vermin-infested she would sue.

This event can and should be revealed now because the statute of limitations has run out and yesterday Luke Shelton's SUV vanished. It is a pearl grey Lexus SUV and Luke had just put on a new set of all-terrain tires with very impressive tread design and raised white letters. He lost it in the Long Plains shopping mall parking lot, and though many people forget where they parked their cars, they ultimately find them again. No such luck for Luke. He did all the things one does when one loses something of this nature in this fashion. He walked up and down the rows of parked cars. He called Hank's Toe-M, thinking he had inadvertently parked in a handicapped spot or fire lane and had been towed away. They said no, and so next he phoned the police. Having little else to do on a Monday morning, the police department sent three patrol cars and a SWAT team to his aid. When they suggested that his SUV might have been stolen, he assured the police, the mall manager, three cart-boys, and a pizza delivery girl, that the Lexus, an otherwise excellent vehicle, could

58

not be started without knowing its ignition secret which consisted of, with key inserted and turned, a small kick had to be directed at the fuse box while the cigarette lighter was fully pushed in. Why this particular Lexus, purchased like-new from the famously trustworthy Old Bill's Automotive Luxury Store, had developed this particular quirk at 40,000 miles was baffling but manageable and so was lived with. Where the Lexus had gone was at least as baffling, but could not be lived with.

Exasperated, but always ready to please at election time, the police chief, after encircling the parking lot with yellow warning tape, called in a psychic who had worked with the department on several prior crimes. Huldah Claire Voyant fingered various pools of oil and antifreeze and solemnly announced that the Lexus, completely stripped, would be found the following spring near a pond or lake or roadway by a stand of trees or line of bushes either outdoors or parked in a garage.

"Things just don't disappear," said Mary when she was six and her new mittens were nowhere to be found.

"Things just don't disappear," said Mary's archeology professor just before leaving for a dig in the Congo. Though he promised to send her a card, she has yet to hear from him.

So Mary Larkin and the Shelton brothers are left asking, "Why don't things just disappear?" Isn't it the case that the Shelton brothers, recent New York transplants and co-directors of Yellowstone Added Value Industries, have no idea where the enormous sums of money they had invested in Montana Power and Light went when the company tanked? Isn't it at least entertainable that some things just go out of existence once in a while? Since objects appear, why not admit that they can also disappear? Has not everyone heard the saying, "It is difficult to keep up appearances these days?"

In the American West the buffalo have vanished. In the nineteenth century there were vast herds, and the song title "Where Have All the Buffalo Gone" captures the conundrum perfectly. Yes, some went to make coats, others to make hats, and still others became deck chair throws. But this can only account for a small percentage of buffalo. Even those old time pictures of buffalo hunts, buffalo shot from train windows by what passed for hunters, cannot account for the phenomenon. This would be like saying that the suburban spread of New York, Chicago, Atlanta, and Los Angeles ultimately caused the Montana lumber industry to disappear.

The point is that lost items go from somewhere to somewhere else, but vanished items go from somewhere to nowhere else. Ultimately, with enough perseverance one can find the somewhere where lost items go. Yet when an item goes nowhere, searching nowhere only turns up nothing. Yes, conspiracy addicts have tried discussing this thesis with government agencies famous for losing things forever, such as the Nuclear Regulatory Commission and the U.S. postal service. Many postmen are well aware that mail disappears, but they have been ordered by superiors to keep quite for fear people would stop using the U.S. mails for anything but advertising circulars and mail order catalog distribution.

Should Mary, the Shelton brothers, and so many others suspect a cover-up or just that humans cannot or will not acknowledge the obvious? Maybe lost keys are disconcerting enough without adding to it that they simply vanished? But then again, would not it save a lot of time and consternation, if one just kept a second set in the drawer and simply admit the keys have vanished and not waste all that time searching for something you may or may not find behind couch cushions, at the bottom of the washing machine tub, in the laundry basket, somewhere in the kitty litter box, behind the milk carton in the refrigerator, on the third shelf of the medicine cabinet, or stuck in the front door lock? Just say they have vanished, and if they turn up later, whether a few minutes, a few days, or just before you are making out you organ donor card, good, and leave it at that—glad that the item in question has finally returned from nowhere.

MOSES GOLDSTEIN'S FORM CHRISTMAS LETTER

Friends,

Jingle Bells and happy holidays to you from me and all the Goldsteins, wife Miriam (not a day older), daughter Scout (growing like a weed) and our new delight, baby Sam at seven pounds eleven ounces. May this note find you happy and healthy. Sorry that you are unable to spend the holiday with us— we know how much you would enjoy a few days in the country. A heavy snow fell last week and the mountains above our little home are crystals and diamonds in the sun. Along Indian Hawk Creek the bushes and trees are frosted wedding veils. Several deer have ventured from the pines to take the feed Scout put out for them.

My legal practice continues to expand. I know some people are angry that I am defending the Neo-Nazi Party of the Greater Northwest Homeland for the Pure White, but everyone has a right to justice. Even though I lost the cases, I thought I did quite well representing the Posse Comitatus and the Montana Free Men. Why I didn't get the Unibomber trial I'll never know. Well, you can't win 'em all, though at times I feel like I am playing out *To Kill A Mockingbird*.

I will guess that you read about the multi-vehicle pile-up on US 93 a few days ago. No one really knows why the first car in the chain reaction spun about and flipped over into oncoming traffic, but the driver did mumble something before dying about several deer appearing out of nowhere and crossing the road. I suppose with all that ice on the highway, the fifteen cars and that gasoline tanker truck had no chance of stopping. We could hear the explosion from the tanker up here at the cabin. You know, it was the worst accident we've had here in God's country since last Christmas when the pile-up was twenty cars and Saint Paul Freebolt's tractor. The accident melted a lot of the snow, but at least it didn't start the sort of forest fires we had to contend with last summer.

Our family continues on its joyous adventure through life always looking forward to an even brighter future. We are not sure why Emperor Jack died, and though we are not saying anything to Scout, Miriam thinks that his broken back was the result of Scout jumping from the barn ladder and landing on him. Emperor Jack was a very good dog and though Miriam disagrees, I do not think the weakness he showed for several days before his untimely death was caused by the rat poison the Raddich's encircle their property with.

Anyway the fractures in Scout's left leg are healing nicely and it will soon be as good as it ever was. I wish you could have heard her buddies at the 4-H club's Christmas party when they greeted her with a rousing "And God bless tiny Tim."

Excellent news on the marriage front. Having found out the financial cost of even an uncontested divorce, Miriam has decided not to leave me.

Every morning I get up thanking God for another day of life. We all took in that must-see blockbuster *The Passion of the Christ* and have converted. No more humanist Judaism for us! We now spend our Sundays at the Great God Almighty Invincible Church over in Hamilton. Having found Christ, I now realize that he died for my sins and my conscience is finally free from that touch of gonorrhea I gave to Miriam when we were dating so many years ago.

Like most of the parishioners at the Great God Almighty Invincible Church, Pastor Bill, we fondly call him "PassthaBilious," is deeply concerned about abortion-on-demand and now gay marriage. He is terribly overweight and his recent bouts of depression don't help much. We are all praying for him and that news about him caught naked with the Shelton brothers and Mary Larkin above Bigelow's Tavern no one believes no matter what the police report says. He is a married man who votes moral values and most importantly he is a Real Christian. Aren't his Sunday sermons always about sin and George W.?

Speaking of Bush, remember Sheriff McNellie? He is out beating the bushes looking for people to join a citizens' posse to track the aliens who are making the crop circles and are disemboweling cattle at the Henderson spread. The Hendersons simply couldn't keep up making all those cakes, pies, and cookies, and those little Xeroxed flying saucers they were selling to all the sight-seers. Things are going to be a lot harder for them now that one of the disemboweled steers was found to have had a picture of the Jesus on its hide.

The Larkins just received their son's last letter from Iraq. It's funny to read how well he is doing and then get a letter from Rumsfeld expressing his sorrow over Abel's death. John and Marta could be sad, but after speaking with Pastor Bill and always keeping in the forefront of their minds scenes from *The Passion of the Christ*, they know that their son has been called home to heaven, a much finer place than Baghdad, and one day he will be resurrected. When Abel faces the Last Judgment, he will stand tall as a Real Christian and true American patriot.

Well, we hope that your Christmas day finds you as happy and joyous as our celebration finds us. As you can tell, life remains pleasant in the mountains of Montana; no worries about drive-by shootings, crack epidemics, inadequate schools, and corruption at the highest levels of government (ha! ha!). Sorry, but the smell of freshly baked gingerbread and mincemeat pie calls me to our kitchen. Remember to keep us in your prayers and remind your Jewish and Muslim friends to please keep Christ in Christmas.

Your friends in Montana,
Miriam, Scout, Sam, and Moses

ELLI STEAMSPRING, MULTI-TASKER

Unable to multi-task, Elli Steamspring committed suicide. She killed herself by running repeatedly into the gingerbread man painted on the brick wall that was the left side of Peterson's Full Sugar Bakery. She ran, bounced back, and ran again, so rapidly that passers-by were unable to grab her. The whole event, which lasted roughly five minutes, looked liked some animal mating ritual, except that Ellie was ramming into the gingerbread man instead of courting him. Peterson's Full Sugar Bakery's chief baker Luke Aphisk, who was in the alley chain smoking, jumped in his car, got his camcorder, and captured the last three minutes of Ellie's protracted but successful suicide. When CNN said that they did not want the footage, Aphisk sent it to "Funniest Home Videos," which awarded him the $1000 grand prize. Aphisk, fully aware of the importance of Ellie's role in winning the prize, graciously offered Mark Ridge, the town mortician and crack addict, half the money to help pay for Ellie's funeral.

Montana, all too rapidly becoming urban, still tries to retain that small town spirit of people helping people, over the backyard fence neighborliness, and tight community. So Ellie Steamspring will never be alone, even if she cannot get into heaven with others in her family because she was a suicide. Nevertheless, the friendly folks of Whitefish have been driven to bizarre behavior simply because the urbanization of the landscape has brought with it multi-tasking, and most Montanans are unable to multi-task though on occasion they find themselves doing two jobs at the same time. Montanans are well aware that they are handicapped, unable to keep up with big city urbanites who multi-task 24-7, but of course the latter have had years of practice.

It was his inability to multi-task that drove Mark Ridge to crack. A trusted Whitefish councilman, a stalwart fund raiser for the Community Chest, and always the first to round up money for Jerry's Kids, when Morticians International ordered its membership to get cell phones, and city council members began wearing pagers, and the Community Chest required its fund raisers to have home answering machines, and Jerry's Kids turned to email, for Mark an immoderate devotion to illegal drugs was the answer.

Since it never made the ten p.m. news, because KTVS' CEO and a long time friend of Mark's father, J. Wright Samuelsen, graciously suppressed the footage, few knew of Mark's arrest. However, according to the police account, it took four officers to pull Mark down from atop the Milvian Bridge where he stood completely addled, shouting that he saw a glowing cell phone in the sky calling repeatedly, "Get with the program, fella." Mark died not long after that when one humid evening as he was sobbing uncontrollably into a recently deceased's coffin, the bronze lid slammed down on his head, killing him instantly.

Luke Aphisk's wife, Martha, is an exceptional woman. She is one of the few in Whitefish who can multi-task, and their four-year old daughter, Marta, multi-tasks as if she was born with a palm pilot in her mouth. All Luke can do is stand back while his wife drives their daughter to Happy Diapers Montessori Pre-School while breakfasting on a drive-thru latte and a Hardee's breakfast burger while on her cell phone to her daughter's ballet teacher about the color of the tutu that is to be sewn by Friday night. After daughter is installed at Happy Diapers, Martha reviews her presentation to the Whitefish Red Cross chapter while making sure that everything is in order for Marta's birthday party which is to begin at exactly four-fifteen with Bobo Klown and a cake with sparklers designed by Martha and baked by Peterson's Full Sugar Bakery. After the Whitefish Red Cross chapter, it is off to sell real estate, then a power lunch at the Catch n' Release Café with a visiting environmentalist from Seattle, wrapping Marta's birthday presents, the birthday party and unwrapping the presents (Bobo Klown was eleven and a half minutes late because he could not manage the car's global position device), Pilates, coaching soccer practice, putting Marta to bed, and then seven minutes speaking lovingly to husband Luke while checking cell-phone messages, cleaning off email spam, reading the *New York Times* home page, and practicing yoga. Luke, completely exhausted watching his wife, falls asleep at ten, and though he records his wife's frenzied activities sequentially, because she is a thoroughly accomplished multi-tasker, in post-modern fashion she can, in any order, forward in time, backward in time, or in a blur of no time at all, work the daily grind. Viewing herself as an indispensable part of the professional class, with no end in sight she goes on multi-tasking through two-thirds of the night. About three a.m. she remembers that she forgot to take Marta to her kindergarten entrance exam tutor.

Luke bakes cakes, cupcakes, cookies, and pies. He is good at strudel and has tried his hand at French pastry. Up to date, he has mastered Tiramisu. When he was just a baker's apprentice, a young woman walked into the shop

who was multi-tasking before it caught on, and he liked her. The affair ended disastrously when he learned that her multi-tasking included the captain of the University of Montana football team, the team's coach, and the mascot who preferred to remain in his mascot costume. Luke is a gifted bakery chef; he works from early morning to afternoon, the long-established baker's schedule; but he simply is unable to multi-task. Put a cell-phone to his ear, and Luke would accidentally switch the blender to high speed and splatter batter throughout the kitchen.

About a month before J. Wright Samuelsen wandered off into the Bob Marshall wilderness, she began blaming her father for her failures at multi-tasking tasks. Judith's father was never able to multi-task, at least not multi-task properly. For him it was like coming over from the old country and trying to learn English. Maybe it was that he had come over from the old country or just that multi-tasking would never appeal to Norwegians, and people simply went about doing no more than two things at once. Before Judith wandered off never to return, she certainly seemed sane enough.

Judith's father had helped out at the Missoula soup kitchen during the Great Depression and later in life, even though busy as the district attorney, "the Legal Eagle of Whitefish," never missed a Sunday playing his trumpet at the Lutheran church on Christ and Main. Judith loved her father: there was candy on Valentine's Day, a very special present at Christmas, and he was always up to family outings on the Fourth of July and Labor Day. But Judith's father never multi-tasked, and so never passed on the gift to his daughter.

And if Bobo Klown's mother was to be faulted, it was Anita Klown's devotion to the 1950s. The house was orderly, the clothes were clean and pressed, and at breakfast, lunch, and supper, there was Jell-O. Conversation might turn to Eisenhower's golf scores, but it would be trumped by a discussion of the newest flavor of Jell-O. If the black-listing of communists came up it was in the context of why there was no licorice Jell-O. There was lime Jell-O with bits of celery, cherry Jell-O with sections of mandarin orange, orange Jell-O with pieces of maraschino cherries, grape Jell-O with peeled grapes. When Monsignor O'Neill came for Sunday tea, or the Mary Magdalene ladies auxiliary, or the Virgin Mary Unwed Mothers Society, there was Jell-O molded and shimmering, flecked with walnut bits, carrot shreds, cottage cheese, and maybe one or two ultimately unspecifiables.

The problem was that Anita Klown, as involved in community activity as she was, did one job at a time, and finished them one job at a time without a planner, sticky notes, or palm pilot. Maybe Anita had faults, but Bobo, his sister Lisa, and his father never saw them. Yes, there was the time when the ladies auxiliary complained about how Anita dressed for the church New Year's Eve party in 1972, but she never quite understood disco and so maybe her velour stretch suit was a bit too tight for ample breasts, but her husband liked it.

No one in Whitefish believes that mothers or fathers should be blamed for their children's failures. Yet here were Ellie, Luke, Mark, and Judith driven to all forms of extreme behavior and so the question must be asked, "Why?" And, of course, the answer must be that Montana has all too rapidly become post-modern, up-to-date, high rise and handsome, and this simply is not the way things used to be.

However, Ellie, Luke, Mark, and Judith are not alone, even if they could not get into heaven because of their inability to multi-task. Many Montanans are unable to multi-task though on occasion they find themselves doing two jobs at the same time. Montanans are well aware that they suffer from a serious handicap, unlike so many of big city dwellers who multi-task 24-7 with one hand tied behind their backs. Recently, an article in *Newsweek* highlighted several Montanans who sat by their fireplace all evening reading a book.

THE THONG CORPORATION

The 1960s brought the Great Sexual Revolution, and like so many Paul Lunes was on its frontlines. As is the case with revolutions, it is difficult to say what spark ignited it and what fanned the flames (two trite expressions, nevertheless so apropos), but Paul would guess the birth control pill, the Women's Liberation Movement, the Free Love Movement, the Viet Nam War, the *Playboy* Philosophy, and the availability of the Velanucci sisters and Betty Goldstein just up the block at the Phi Pi Omicron sorority house. As for Paul's wife to be, by sheer good luck it would be many years before they would meet.

In 1967 Paul received a personal letter from the government of the United States of America inviting him to a free physical examination, which if passed, entitled him to an all-expense-paid tour of the more thrilling portions of Southeast Asia. Like so many other young men eager to serve their country, Paul immediately thought of how much he would miss the pleasures, provided by the young women who were serving the young men of the free-love '60s if he accepted the invitation. Paul also considered that if he were ever to settle down and marry, he might already be dead.

As a soldier Paul would carry a rifle, maybe a grenade or two, and a personal medical kit containing among other necessities, three condoms. Upon encountering the enemy he would kill the bastard, knowing that his prophylactic was protecting him from any of the many venereal diseases all enemies of the American Way carry. Then again, if the enemy were female, maybe Paul was to first have sex with her and then kill her or at least take her captive so he might have more sex later. Why else three condoms? Only a soldier knows what it is like crouching in a foxhole with bayonet and condom affixed.

Viet Nam ended before Moses Goldstein, Betty's strange little brother, got a chance to be issued a rifle, some grenades and his condoms, and he was happy at law school when the Balkans, Somalia, Desert Storm, Afghanistan, and Iraq took 'Nam's place. It was during these shining years of America's intercourse with other nations, that the membership of the Genuine Patriot

Sexual Repression League, not wishing to miss out on all the fun, but not sure about traveling in uncivilized lands with their aluminum walkers, opened up the home front with the Lawrence Welk Sexual Repression Police Action. Here was a massive effort aimed at the minds and reproductive organs of Americans who could be divided between morally upright, law-abiding, family-oriented, God fearing patriots and liberal perverts. After Moses sexually transmitted a sexually transmitted disease to his wife to be, and someone else whose name he never really got, there was no doubt where he stood.

Some blame war on the discovery by the Women Are Made Not Born Movement that all that men wanted was sex. Some blame the Nietzsche was Pietzsche Movement's claim that all that women want is a clean kitchen and babies. Some blame the ever-expanding panoply of sexually transmitted diseases (STD International) that demanded that possible copulaters first recite the sex-ed teacher's mantra, "Before falling victim to your animal drives, know the other animal's sexual history." This is like going into battle and inquiring of the fellow you want to shoot if he ever killed, wounded, scared, or simply annoyed anyone. Still others blame the Genuine Patriot Sexual Repression League itself, with their battle cry of "Billions of rabbits died for your sins." Wherever the Genuine Patriots were victorious, lovers got down on bended knee before touching each other's exciting parts and thanked America's Founding Fathers (except for Thomas Jefferson) for the gifts one was about to receive. The truly converted never failed to remind each other that sex is only for procreation of patriots and not a splendid terminus to a great evening.

About this time into Moses' life came Miriam Rosen, who is better described as Moira Moonstone. She was transmitting no diseases, sexual or otherwise, at least none that could be clinically detected; only read Nietzsche once every four years on February 29; and was born not made. Miriam was an advertising executive whose accounts included The Thong Corporation (the Billings, Montana, jackhammer and steam drill consortium founded by the Helen Thong), Buffalo Chip Bricks, and Road Kill Financial Services. Miriam had a wonderful, professionally trained smile that could smile at fate and Moses' weak attempt to begin a conversation, engaging or otherwise, with someone to whom he had just been introduced but had already forgotten the name.

They met at the Third Annual Montana Added Value Convention. Since it was readily apparent that Miriam was stranger than Moses, an opener like "Odd weather we're having lately" was a non-starter. Worse yet, law school had forced Moses to miss out on the wonders of crystal power and disco nights. Treated with delicacy, sex and the behaviors it inspires might be a good topic unless one is in conversation with a nun or a Genuine Patriot, which at the Convention banquet where Moses was seated next to Miriam, there may or may not have been any. Suddenly, he began to think that maybe a conversation about condoms, citing their use and abuse, might be engaging, but then he reconsidered. Nevertheless, as if reading his mind, across the table, Thong Corporation CEO, Irving Thong, son of Helen, brought up what he must have thought an appropriate ice-breaker, but Miriam appeared less than impressed when he began his dissertation on the various sizes, colors, textures, lubricants, packaging, and prices of the modern prophylactic. It was one of those times Moses was glad that he had thought before he spoke, and later that evening he learned that Miriam could bring into being the most glorious acts of sexual gratification as Moira Moonstone.

HOSANNA WRIGHT, LOVER

Dear Secret Passion,

Yes, I'm aware that personal letters should be hand written, but after working a keyboard for decades I have forgotten my cursive. Yes, I can jot down a word or two in some sort of recognizable script, words like "milk," "bread," "whipping cream," even "2 pair handcuffs," but that is the extent of it.

Do you find this strange? . . . I do not. I can no longer add unless a calculator is in reach. And, I, like you, have forgotten how to cook because of those damned microwaves. Make coffee? Hit the switch. Ask me if I remember how to wash dishes. Well, you put them in the dishwasher and press a button.

Nevertheless, it is true that I no longer can play a record or CD or snap pictures. Maybe you've phoned, but I do not answer my answering machine because I can't get it to disgorge messages. These wondrous devices have become so complicated I get terribly depressed whenever their existence is brought up in conversation. Just what is a mega-pixel and how is it related to either string theory or string cheese? After six months I did master the television remote, but I still feel not as if I have fallen with Alice down the rabbit hole, but into a post-modern, possibly post mortem, black hole.

And as for desktop, laptop, or palm pilot, I can do no more than word process and vilify, along with everybody else at the water cooler, those damn kids and their blasted viruses. In moments of exquisite delirium, I have imagined that Satan is housed in my CPU.

Anyway, my days continue their valiant attempt to calm the frenzy that you so generously gave me. Maybe I should exhaust myself in Rome. Maybe I should go to Paris and romance a string of beautiful women. I have heard that the Andalusian girls are without equal. I have been reading about Islam and wonder what is really going on behind those veils and beneath those turbans. Next time, would you come veiled?

It is Saturday night, and I don't feel much like typing, but even if I have finally mastered the remote, I couldn't locate it after returning from the bathroom, and the second hand hot tub I bought last spring isn't heating up or bubbling or doing much of anything except acting like a big ice bucket, and the dog spilled the last of the Chardonnay on the carpet, and the Internet is down, and a folder of lecture notes went missing a few weeks ago as did my husband, and I know that there must be a Country & Western song in this somewhere, because this is Basin, population five saloons, a gas station, and a church of some nondescript denomination. But the stars are magnificent here, because there are no streetlights, and after ten the police chief turns off the flashing yellow light where Main crosses Gunstock. It isn't Paris or Rome or Berlin, but I know you'd like it. Come to me.

For the last five minutes I have been giving serious consideration to going to sleep and Columbus Day. Of course everyone knows that Columbus thought he had discovered Cathay, not Havana, which is similar to what happened when I was in the tenth grade and I discovered Susan Havana. All the way to the lunchroom and then to the girl's bathroom, I kept calling her Cathy, because her algebra book had "This book belongs to Cathy" on it, and I didn't learn until spring break that Susan had borrowed Cathy's book, though this didn't make any difference because both Susan and Cathy thought I was an idiot. So Susan Havana, who may or may not have been from Cuba or China or any other place beyond Billings, stole my heart and promptly sold it to this three-letter jock who like Susan and Cathy had a big, endless laugh at my expense.

I only got over that disaster when my second book, (the one I was speaking from when I saw you in the audience), became an international best seller or at least made me some money. Before that time the Susan Havana-Cathy Cuba Affair was only one of so many arising from my attempts at interpersonal relations with a sex that appeared as willing as mine. Yes, I dated anyone who would have me, and perused videos with titles like *When Your First Date Is Your Last* and *Why the Motel was Invented*. Nothing helped and so I have remained single until I met you even though I got married just about seven years ago now. It follows that I am a lover, though on more than several occasions in several Basin bars, my husband has refused to acknowledge this. It's a cruel world, and I suppose we all did something, or at least I did, to deserve it.

Write. Please write. It would be so good and great to hear from you. I do not wish to be indelicate, but please don't forget that the Paris conference was followed by a week of sex-drenched nights. So now I must go and get that thing we bought. Maybe that will put me to sleep; I only need to push the one button—that I know how to do.

In obsession,
Hosanna

RADON MINES AND REACTIONARIES

Being semi-arid and dry, Montana is overrun by water-witchers who for a small fee are ready and willing to guide well-diggers to water. No matter if the douser uses nothing more than a forked birch stick, or the more expensive copper dowels, water-witching does not work, but then true believers are never deterred.

There are also people in Montana who sit in played out gold and silver mines to soak up cancerous radon so they can regain their health. Struggling with asthma, arthritis, and other less definable maladies, they sit for hours playing Cribbage or Snooker or Texas Hold-Em, soaking up as much radon as they can get, and then go home to wherever they live.

Every so often someone will immigrate to Montana and build an eight by six shack and spend enormous amounts of time figuring out how to put tiny little bombs in envelopes so that they can mail these to people they do not know but who have done them some terrible injustice. Still others want to bomb the United States government, or at least the local school board because neither will admit that evolution is a hoax and that the world was created in six days.

That God made people like this, and that He did not cut them down just before reaching the age of sanity, only shows that God has a terrific sense of humor even if exactly what is funny is beyond human comprehension.

Driven to action by Joe McCarthy's anti-communist crusade and repeated viewings of *I Led Three Lives*, Belle Anne, Anne Kostelec, Marcus Aurelius Two Feathers, and Jesus Esposito became reactionaries who saw it as their life's work to destroy Bolshevik governments, blow up socialist small-is-beautiful industrial projects, infiltrate Marxist cells, and undermine the hallowed institution of pre-marital sex. They had met in kindergarten and formed a tight bond from the very beginning. In grade school they devised a secret code where A was 1, B was 2, and so on, which only after many tortured hours was broken by Solomon Softsole. In high school they took small arms training. At the Montana Tech School of Mines they learned how to build landmines and mine harbors. Disaster struck but was overcome when Marcus Aurelius blew off the top of his right ear in a freak trick pencil accident while in chemistry class. Another time Anne's vibrator broke while she was explaining to Belle the finer points of undercover intelligence gathering.

On July 4, 1952, Action Group Alphalpha staged a daring ten p.m. raid on the Billings Furniture Mart which had just closed its doors on a most successful Independence Day furniture sale featuring one percent interest loans to World War II veterans and Korean GIs. The owner, surprised while going through receipts, was duct taped to the cleaning lady and then both were herded into the men's room at the rear. An under-the-dash hot-wired black moving van was backed up to the loading dock, and within minutes the store's entire sofa and love seat collection complete with their protective plastic covers had been loaded. Everything was then driven to the Great Falls Hock and Haunch, and the cache was pawned for ten cents on the dollar. The next day the Montana Highway Patrol had roadblocks across the state, but by this time the truck was back at Humpin' to Please Transfer and Storage in Cascade, the paint had been washed away, and Action Group Alphalpha was scattered among the shoppers at the Saturday morning open air market in Missoula.

The Independence Day operation was followed by a well-coordinated series of gas station raids. Jake's Conoco was hit as was Hank's Sonoco and Tilly's Pit Stop. Action Group Deltoid's MO was identical, except that when the gas station attendant at Jake's finished checking the oil, he forgot to clean the windshield. It could be that he noticed that the black paint was water soluble and so did not want to get any of his window spray on the hood.

The next raid was on Thanksgiving just after "We Close Early" sales, when Action Group Gamete struck the Billings IGA Super Market. Again the MO was identical, except that this time the bag boy in aisle six put up a terrible struggle and finally had to be subdued by jumping on him after he reached for the O'Henry's that had been tossed on the floor. Duct tape, blacked out truck, and the boxes of nickel candy bars and bags of chips were loaded, then unloaded fifty-three minutes later for cash at the Stuckey's just north of where 27th Street crossed US 212. Years later when I-90 was put through, one of twelve historical markers marked that stage of the daring feat.

The final raid came on Christmas Eve. Action Group Lazy Boy Decliner staged a daring midnight hit on the Bob Ward's Hunting and Fishing Superstore in Helena. Some of the take ended up in the hands of juvenile delinquents who were future reform and military school rebels without a cause.

Of course Alphapha, Deltoid, Gamete, and Lazy Boy Decliner were respectively each headed by Belle Anne, Anne Kostelec, Marcus Aurelius

Two Feathers, and Jesus Esposito, now known by her or his *nom de guerre* as Washington, Jefferson, Adams, and Monroe. And of course, with the money made from pawnshops and it fell-off-the-truck merchandise transfers, fake passports, disguises, hush money, payoffs to ships' captains, and various tools of the reactionary's trade were purchased.

Then on Easter Sunday 1951 the fatalistic four and their followers rendezvoused on Cemetery Island, a small isle in the Missouri River not far from where Louis and Clark had camped on their way to discovering that Indians, buffalo, and bear would make great targets for settlers moving West. The Missouri was now much wider because of the dam, and Cemetery Island had actually been the high and dry cemetery of the prosperous town of Resurrection before the river was turned into a lake.

The band of guerrillas began to prepare for their assault on North Korea and the ultimate overthrow of its dictatorship. Training was even more intense than for the raids that had been staged across Montana. They made contact with Kate Smith, George M. Cohan, and Red Buttons, real Americans, but were unable to secure their services. Thinking that J. Edgar Hoover might be tapping their telephone, the group corresponded either face to face or by carrier pigeon. However, because of their silence-till-death code, little is known of their training and the actual details of the planned invasion and subsequent overthrow of the North Korean government.

What is known is that in the final stages of preparation for their assault their code was cracked by Solomon Softsole of the Butte FBI office. It seems that he had intercepted a carrier pigeon that had became disoriented in a freak mid-June windstorm. Working night and day, he deciphered, "NK invasion prep on schedule." Supposing that North Korea was planning to invade Montana, Softsole's superiors clipped a homing device on the pigeon's left leg and put a fake message back into the capsule on its right. After the storm had passed, the pigeon was sent on its way, tracked, of course, by the FBI and other covert government operatives.

Fortunately for Washington, Jefferson, Adams, and Monroe, the FBI mistakenly attacked the Rest for Eternity Cemetery just off Missouri Boulevard. The Helena Police Department, notified that vandals were shooting at tombstones, drove out and in a show of force subdued the FBI agents. Catching an agent with cyanide capsule mid-throat, Sergeant Custer, who had been training for just such an eventuality since his boa choked to death on a hamster, swiftly administered the Heimlich maneuver, thereby winning the highly coveted Nice Cop Of the Year Award at the annual Officers Recognition Dinner. However, hearing the machine gun fire and grenades all the way out on Cemetery Island, the young reactionaries of Capitalism, Democracy, and Black Listing guessed that their days of rage were over.

Belle Anne, Anne Kostelec, Marcus Aurelius Two Feathers, and Jesus Esposito have since moved on. No longer friends, their union suffered after a vicious argument over whether to become the Mamas and the Papas or ABBA. Washington and Adams became Tammy Wynette and George Jones. Jefferson married D.C. Lukovich and opened Lukovich's Television and Appliance Store in Butte. And Jesus Esposito ended his days surrounded by well-wishers after being magnificently gored by a magnificent bull after jumping into and then circling several times the Correro del Toro in Madrid.

JOE TUNSDALE III'S TERM PAPER

Joe Tunsdale III's term paper was to be an analysis of Isaac Newton's claim that space and time are the constants of the universe. Knowing that his report was due at 10:00 a.m. Joe did not ask for whom the bell tolls or when, and so he was staying up all night writing.

In the room next door, disaster struck at 4:30 a.m. when Alma Armstrong's laptop kept flashing "error" as she repeatedly tried to enter "Einstein concluded that space and time are relative, which implies that . . . ." Alma saw the little paper clip fellow on her Windows XP screen transfigure into the Grim Reaper.

If there is one thing certain about contemporary life, it is that there is never enough time to get everything done that has to be done. Whether relative or not time marches on, no one has time on their hands anymore, and there is not always time to get a research paper, term paper, essay, company report, or editorial done or to say, "I love you." Therefore, it came as a relief when Marla Slenska, who was just at www.wowfacts, ran down the dorm hallway past Joe's door and into Armstrong's room yelling that a certain Professor Hans Abscurskii had demonstrated in 1950 that time is unreal. Upon overhearing, Joe immediately thought of his grandfather whom too many had also thought unreal.

Here were three little words fashioning the finest labor-saving device ever given to humankind, for if there is no time, there is no time to start, work at, or finish all those projects that cannot possibly get done in the time available. "Time is unreal" was the central thesis, the linchpin, the cornerstone and keystone of a philosophical opus that Abscurskii developed and maintained through decades of philosophical speculation, and there is no telling how many people around the world took him seriously. Years before Marla Slenska ran down the dorm hallway, the Grandfather clock that stood in Abscurskii's bedroom, a clock his grandfather had purchased the day Hans was born, miraculously stopped working the exact second Hans' posthumously published book, *The Non-Existence of Yesterday, Today and Tomorrow* pushed Martin Heidegger's *Being and Time* (revised) off the *New York Times* best seller list. Abscurskii was ninety-six when he drowned.

Red Fishburn, a whitewater rafting guide out of Fishburn, Montana, was one of the first to take Abscurskii at his word. When Abscurskii's insight reached the brilliant University of Montana biologist, Lawrence FitzWilliam, in 1955, the young Fitzwilliam with his almost completed theory of the double helix was on his way to winning the Nobel Prize, but depressed by the thought that there would be no 1956 in which to be nominated and possibly win the Nobel Prize, he immediately terminated his research. He moved to the timeless landscape of northwest Montana, Fishburn to be exact, changed his name to Red Fishburn, and became a whitewater rafting guide. Watson and Crick, who had not read Abscurskii's paper, or if they had, did not understand it, took the Nobel Prize home.

Abscurskii's thesis produced innumerable Fishburns over the next years. Lisa Marie Daniels stopped hosting Tupperware parties because they took up time she did not have. Mariah Pietrukowicz auctioned off her Avon cosmetics franchise at a local home for unwed mothers one afternoon. Isaiah and Bethany Warhook, successful day traders, when they learned that days did not exist jumped from a third floor window at the Billings Stock and Bond Exchange and were never seen or heard from again. And millions of Americans breathed a sigh of relief knowing that the far too little money they had put away for retirement they could spend now since those years would never come.

But as with every other revolutionary insight or at least the ones that make the pages of *People* magazine or *Reader's Digest*, the world divided into many camps, and soon rational discourse failed, epithets were hurled, and mayhem erupted in the United Nations General Assembly. Lists of late arrivals and departures at airports jettisoned their vagueness and simply became meaningless. Suicide bombers tore at their dynamite vests distraught that the right time to murder would never come. Terrorists at late night Great Apocalyptic Bull Sessions smashed their watch crystals and steamed over their glasses torturing each other over the uselessness of their time bombs. Fights broke out while waiting in lines at county fair port-o-potties where minutes can seem like hours.

It was 3:26 a.m. and Joe Tunsdale III's term paper was not finished, and then Alma Armstrong, whom he did not like, stopped to say she was just about done. "Good for you" was all Joe could manage as he turned back to his report wondering what website would sell him what he needed at 3:30.

So, Joe Tunsdale III, Alma Armstrong, and Jon Johannsen, who had just remembered he, too, had a research paper due, knew that God existed when Marla Slenska ran down the dorm hallway past Joe's door and into Armstrong's room yelling, "Time is unreal. Time is unreal."

Could this be? Could this really be? Could the real world actually be penetrating college dormitory life, crowded as it is with I-Pods, X-Boxes, and posters of Leonardo DiCaprio and Britney Spears. The conversation skewed to Abscurskii, Einstein, and Newton, and in the heat of discussion the minutes flew by. Around 5:30 a.m., just about the time roosters start thinking about getting the sun out of bed, Joe and company began losing contact with reality. They had broken the wall clock as they inspected what made it tick, and Jon's Fossil had been hurled against a bedroom cabinet. By 6:45 Joe, Alma, and Jon had moved from discussion to obsession to frenzy to the campus dining hall for breakfast. Time after time Abscurskii was shown wrong, then right, and then it was Newton's turn to be followed by Einstein.

Sometime around noon, Joe and company showed up at Hosanna Wright's office. They showed up with half-finished papers, claiming that they had no time to finish them. As they began to speak of Abscurskii, Professor Wright marked each paper "late" and "minus ten." Alma protested that time was unreal and therefore the papers could not possibly be late. Wright did not appear to be listening.

But Joe, Alma, and Jon's cause was soon taken up by other students, and soon students said that if the issue were not resolved in favor of the students, lawyers would be hired and the college would face a class action suit. Though the protest spread, it took several weeks to reach the president of the college, who had been scouring Bali beaches looking for donors. It did not take long until the president, after consulting with the Board of Trustees and the woman he had been seeing, realized that more important than questions of time or academics were questions of money. In their combined wisdom, the president and Board agreed time was unreal, and for their insight, Joe and company regained their lost ten points and the Board promised the president a raise in salary if he kept the affair quiet.

As for Red Fishburn, he died in a rafting accident mere minutes after reading about Abscurskii's passing. Hosanna Wright is considering the sound of "Wright's Whitewater Adventures."

LISA DANIELS, SIZE MEANS EVERYTHING

Most Montana males and fewer but still a sizable number of females think that voluminous breasts are erotic. Many Montanans also think that Velveeta is cheese. Researchers have shown in study after study that there exists a substantial overlap between people who think Velveeta is cheese and people who find enormous breasts erotic.

Velveeta on Ritz as football tailgate party hors d'oeuvres goes nicely with those red, white, and somewhere-in-between half-gallon cartons of trailer court wine. Software executives, millionaire plastic surgeons, and tax lawyers, all recent transplants from New York, Los Angeles, and Chicago, will leave their Cadillac Escalade, Lexus, or Mercedes SUV in the garage and crowd college football stadium parking lots with rented Ford 150s, Chevy Built Like a Rock but rusty Silverados, Jeeps, and dented Jimmies. Desirous of being mistaken for real Montanans, the ones they have come to know so well from The History Channel or the pages of old *National Geographic*s, the nouveau riche nouvelle cuisine immigrants go slumming in pickup trucks nicely outfitted with a big dog or two, over-sized tires, an air freshener dangling from the mirror, and a rifle rack. Tailgates overflowing with endless varieties of chili and chips under melted Velveeta, men stand around with a beer in hand and the talk is of quarterbacks, fullbacks, and point spread while they survey for a possible pick-up that is weighted down with enormous breasts. The milieu here is one with which Dolly Parton and the Dallas cheerleaders could easily identify.

It is beautiful fall day, but it could not be Anywhere, USA, because only in Montana can people actually keep rifles stacked in the truck rifle rack. It is a fall day in Missoula, and the Griz are going to fight the Bobcats, or the Hawks or Griffins or Eagles, and for Montanans, native or newly made, size does make a difference. But no matter the intensity of the betting over the size of the point spread, the Montana male is never far from dreams of falling like Ritz cracker crumbs into the great chasms created by Victoria Secret push-up bras. He is never far from his dreams of descending into canyons of cleavage created by a Mother Nature run wild. He tumbles with Alice through the looking glass to find a topsy-turvy world where the White Rabbit has mutated into a pneumatic Playboy Bunny. He is enamored of a downside up world where the top heavy instead of sinking rises and spreads skyward. He does not want to be awakened.

Lisa Daniels, exactly like her mother Anita Klown, was stuck in the '50s, and so has mastered hundreds of Jell-O recipes. It goes without saying that her most infamous concoction is the greenish Jell-O mold infused with chunks of Velveeta and sprinkled with the Roni from a package of Rice-a-Roni she made for her husband. Jake, only a month before he choked to his untimely death on a glob of Roni cemented together by semi-melted Velveeta, had become obsessed with Madonna's way of promoting her siliconized breasts, and he began sporting his underwear outside his clothes. Initially, the coroner reported that he died from a ruptured appendix caused by abdominal pressures exacted by the tee-shirt and Jockey shorts he was wearing outside his coveralls when he was hoisting a beer keg onto the flatbed of someone's rented Ford 150 at a tailgate party. Nevertheless, after exhumation a second autopsy found that his wife, by employing the Velveeta-Roni Jell-O, had murdered him. Prosecutors theorized that being a small-breasted woman, Lisa could not tolerate her husband's fixation with the cleavage she, quite unlike her mother, did not have.

Eroticism takes time and study to appreciate—time that multi-tasking Montanans, whether the newly made or native, do not have and study that palm piloting does not offer. Lisa's defense attorney, to Moses Goldstein's credit, pointed out to the jury that she had tried any number of bust-enhancers, but her bosom was in God's hands, and obviously God was not in a generous mood when configuring Lisa's upper torso. In closing arguments Goldstein said something no man should ever forget. He said, "Eroticism is not Pamela Anderson supersized. It is not Pamela Anderson. If anything, erotic must be a state of mind, not the lay of the land."

You betcha!

TALKIN' TRASH

"Kitsch" is not a term of endearment. To call something kitsch is to call it banal, trite, ersatz, imitative, pedestrian, sentimental, shallow, and downright schmaltzy. From whence the word came, no one is quite sure. It may have come from a mistaken rendering of the English "sketch," as in "It's only a sketch, not a serious piece of work." It may be derived from "*kitschen,*" a verb in the Mecklenburg-German dialect meaning, "to make cheap." Or it may come from a German phrase meaning "collecting rubbish from the street."

Just above the bar at the Butte Miners Saloon hangs a nicely framed black velvet open-skirted, spread-legged siren enhanced with day-glo colors. The painting is teamed with a heavily bosomed raven-haired young woman outlined in glitter. The unemployed miners who arrive by eight and leave when the doors close reminisce about better days when the mines were open and the whorehouses were filled with such enticing artwork.

The four identical wall sconces of a gold lamé outfitted Elvis complete with pompadour and guitar at the Lumberman's Café in Missoula have a certain appeal to the college students who gather there on Friday and Saturday nights. Females think the decoration is "qewl," and the brothers from Alpha Tau Omega would steal Elvis if he were not so tightly bolted to the wall.

There is a miniature Lucite spaceship containing simulated moon dust residing in the glass-fronted imitation wood cabinet just outside the Governor's office in the state capitol building. The caption reads, "Replica of Lunar Landing Vehicle with Simulated Moon Dust. Gift of the Thong Corporation. A.D. 1986."

But the finest kitsch display is between Plentywood and Scobey, two Highline towns on the point of vanishing that are trying to attract tourists by erecting plastic dinosaurs. Replacing the Burma Shave signs that stretched between the two towns are what can only be described as twelve Dinosaur-Biblical tableaux. The Plentywood-Scobey promotion committee, to a person convinced that the world is only six thousand years old, commissioned the Extruded Plastics Corporation of Harlowton (a subcontractor for Bighorn Industrials, a tractor fittings and space shuttle interior decoration firm in

Bighorn) to build the scenes. Starting at Plentywood, there is a Tyrannosaurus Rex, always a crowd pleaser, about to be speared by Adam as Eve holds babies Cain and Able. Next is Noah on his Ark with what might be a Stegosaurus or a Triceratops drowning in the background. Circled by high-flying pterodactyls, the Tower of Babel is being built by Neanderthals. Scobey has the singular honor of having God walking between a giant ground sloth and a wooly mammoth just beyond the sign that says "pop.525" and "Rotary Club meets at Fly's Café noon, Mondays."

For the rest of Montanans so inclined, kitsch can be purchased at shopping malls with names like Hill Center, Road Hills, Hill Hollow, Mountain Hollow, and Rockdale. For the folks who are fed up with shopping mall drek, they can renew their souls in the miles of schlock-stocked aisles of Wal-Mart, Kmart, Shopko, and Target.

Of course, Mary, Mary, Martha, and John are hungry after all that shopping. So there are kitsch restaurants in the "food court" with salad bars, make your own sundaes, and buffets with innumerable barely edible Chinese collations. For mealtime entertainment, the Missilettes, a local preschool dance team will perform their rendition of the Radio City Music Hall Rocket's version of *Rodeo* or possibly Rodeo Drive.

Politically involved? It is sound-bite politics, my fellow Americans.

Devout? It is sound-bite sermons. Jesus loves you. Deepak Chopra loves you, too.

Are you concerned? It is Dr. James Dobson alerting the world to Sponge Bob Square Pants' attempts to turn every ten year old into a homosexual pervert. If not Sponge Bob Square pants, beware of Arthur at PBS.

But what is so wonderful about kitsch is though it is awful stuff, it is difficult not to be fascinated by it, even enamored of it, at least in the same way mothers are fascinated by all those mind-bending stories in checkout stand tabloids. Of course, any serious attempt to explain the attraction would move into the realm of complicated philosophical, sociological, and aesthetic theories that would leave the source of such a psychological response more opaque than it is now. However, why should that stop anyone? And so, being true lovers of kitsch, and well-knowing its proper place, Joe Tunsdale, Hosanna Wright, Anita Klown, and Sophia Beets will offer a sound-bite answer:

"We can indubitably assert that I think therefore I am always going to be attracted to that which unabashedly romances my simple soul, which is okay so long as I take this stuff, as I should all things, in moderation. And though kitsch takes itself seriously, I know better, though not much better. You betcha, howzit hangin', and have a nice day."

WHY HUMANS WOULD BE CONFUSED IF THEY CAME FOR A VISIT

With psychologists, sociologists, and a vast array of therapists hard at work trying to discover what makes human beings human, on occasion Luke Aphisk feels guilty when he is in his garden with a cold beer and cigarette watching some birds on their way to somewhere stopping to take a drink from the pond. Sometimes Luke is joined by his friend Bobo Klown, and they talk through the afternoon, irresponsibly failing to resolve what makes them human. Luke knows that his next door neighbor Huldah Voyant, who will one day burn down her house because she will forget to snuff out the three hundred candles and incense sticks she lives with, believes that women should be out there just beyond indefinable human civilization running, if not with wolves, then at least with a deer or two. Bobo, who last fall finally jettisoned his marathon running-around wife, wonders what he would say to alien invaders from the planet Zirconium in the galaxy Velma, who just before they destroy all humanity, ask him what makes humans human.

Is it that psychologists, sociologists, and a vast array of therapists think that if what it is to be human cannot be defined, John or Mary will never know if they are being addressed by a fellow human when some kid at the ballpark says, "Hey, whassup?" As a sometimes-thoughtful creature, Luke is sympathetic to the problem.

Speaking of "thoughtful," Aristotle said that man is the rational animal. It is a good bet that he meant male, not male and female, for the best he could say for women is that they were barely rational men. Far be it from Luke not to have the greatest respect for an author whose works have been read for two thousand years and have driven countless people to spend innumerable hours attempting to understand what he was trying to say. Nevertheless, if Aristotle found women less rational than men he was wrong, for human beings of both sexes and any sexual orientation have proven on far too many occasions to be equally without a shred of rationality, let alone native intelligence or even common sense. Think for a moment, exactly what is the purpose of Hamburger Helper or where is the music in Rap music? You certainly would not find an answer to those burning questions in Aristotle's *Metaphysics*, *De Anima*, or the *Nicomachean Ethics*.

St. Augustine, *paterfamilias* of Medieval Catholicism and Martin Luther's morality, did not think very highly of himself and then projected his depressing assessment onto the rest of humankind. People are vipers waiting to strike, dogs fierce to rut, pig-gluttons stealing from neighbors' pear trees. Sinners, and who is not, will be thrown into Hell's barbecue pit, the carcasses of rotting rats would be stuffed down their throats, and flesh will be flailed raw and really bloody by Mel Gibson. Augustine defines man as a body and soul, filled with Original Sin, but up for salvation, if he gets Satan behind him, puts his faith in Jesus, and a loving Father has him destined for salvation in the great cosmic plan even if the fellow in question had been a mass murderer. And yet, Luke and Bobo cannot help thinking that anyone who goes to such length berating himself, detailing his most petty crimes while failing to reflect on how his perverse outlook would lead to terrible crimes against others, or at least against Jews, is really a misguided soul who has no idea of what constitutes humanity.

William Shakespeare may have done better, if only slightly. "What a piece of work is man/how infinite in faculties/in form and movement how express and admirable/ in movement how like an angel," and then all this collapses into Hamlet's well of despair and who is not left wondering where all the *joie de vivre* is in human beings such as these. Jonathan Swift thought that horses were more human than humans, Gilbert and Sullivan had far too much to say on the subject, and Freud announced that without at least one or two really perverse libidinous thoughts, you would not be a male, and females, lacking a penis of their own, were at best defective men.

The twentieth century has seen humans defined by what social behavior they have adopted. There have been Jazz babies, war veterans, beatniks, hippies, yippies, yuppies, and granolas, liberals, conservatives, fundamentalists, and evangelicals. Of course, there were more philosophical assessments of what it is to be human such as "man the maker" and "woman the homemaker." Then the *Great Falls Tribune* Sunday Literary Supplement informed its readership that human beings were not human beings at all, but actually men are Martians and women, Venusians. Today, there are lots of post-modern young men and women out for self-definition in some multi-cultural deconstructionist fashion, which in the pre-post-modern age were known as people with a Bachelor of Arts degree in English literature.

What any of this has done to better the definition of people who live in Montana's Paradise Valley on estates costing upwards of several million, or people dust farming in the northeastern part of the state or Indians in pre-fabs on the reservations is beyond Luke and Bobo.

Yet, if Luke cannot characterize human beings and spell out their nature, how is he going to know that when Bobo asks "How's everything going today?" he would be responding to a fellow human? All the philosophers and social scientists' hard work almost makes Luke feel guilty when he is in his garden watching the grass grow. Sometimes he is joined by another organism or two, and they talk, none of them quite sure if they are rational or not, if they are even communicating, or if they should not be out there just beyond indefinable human civilization running, if not with wolves, then at least with a deer or two. Luke cannot wait until someone tells him who he is; it will be as exciting as the Human Genome Project, which when he thinks about it, has not helped either.

(The following academic paper was presented at the University of Montana in the fall of 2003 at the twenty-second annual convention of the Sociolobotomy Forum, the premier international organization of sociologists and cultural anthropologists. The paper was the work of Harvard sociologist Susan Mandala Smith, the Rabbi Shaddai Challah, and the native Montanan freelance anthropologist Margaret GoldenHawkFisheyeSpearchucker. It has since been published in the prestigious *Bulletin of Sociological Studies** and excerpted in the *Missoulian*, the Helena *Independent Record*, the Hardin *Star*, Billings *Gazette*, and the Great Falls *Tribune*.)

A POST-STRUCTURAL POST-MODERN ETHNOGRAPHIC STUDY OF THE GRANOLAS OF MONTANA

Drawing on work in the social sciences since the 1990s that has focused on the operation of human agency within structures of subordination, sociologists and cultural anthropologists, working within a post-structural post-modern conceptual framework, have sought to cognize the ways in which the mysterious Granola tribe of northwestern Montana resists the dominant New Yorker and Californian order by subverting the hegemonic meanings of cultural practices and redeploying them for their own interests and agendas. Clearly, this deconstruction is the key to understanding the otherwise opaque Granola religion and its flippant but nevertheless serious rallying cry, "Veggies Rule!"

The Granola tribe, whose origin has been traced back to the free speech, free love, open marriage, Drop City commune, marijuana, and LSD driven culture of the 1960s Hippie Movement,[1] can be further subdivided into a network of clan and family relations, though for the purposes of this study this salient feature is completely without importance. Minor differences among clan orthodoxy, orthopraxy, orthodontics, and the employment of prophylactics can be dismissed, given the centrist (as distinct from peripheral) focus of the present study.

Scholars of the caliber of the UCLA team of Gotmilch, Twinkowitz, and Crunchk (Capt., Royal Grenadiers)[2] have tended to explore cultural traditions in terms of the foundational presuppositions and praxis-oriented resources that post-structural post-modern anthropologists have directed to secure social agendas. This technique now can be employed to uncover the site of the Granola's agency and the closely guarded secret of their essentialist creed.

As Emeril noted in his recently published landmark study, "Granola Power-Avoidance of Sushi Preference and Preferential Treatment,"[3] the innate desire for autonomy and self-expression constitutes a substrate, a slumbering hypo-allergenic organic locus of a sublimated eroticism, that could flame under the recoding of, and thereby marginalizing of, the nationally dominant New Yorker and Californian order as an act of resistance when conditions permit. Emeril, placing his field observations of Granola performance rituals within a post-structural post-modern post-toasties framework[4] grown from the writings of Gotmilch, et al., has succeeded in integrally linking the notion of self-fulfillment with individual autonomy insofar as the process of realizing oneself comes to signify the ability to realize oneself and the desires of one's "true will" and "happy, happy thoughts."[5]

CONCLUSION

By standing on the shoulders of such research giants as Gotmilch, Twinkowitz, Crunchk, and Emeril[6] the authors of this paper are able to conclude that Granolaism is born out of the realization that despite the fact that modernist critiques have been key in decentering reactionary or radical notions of autonomy, voluntarism, and the transcendental subject, the normative supposition of Granola actualization of false-consciousness in consciousness and then its attendant conscious rejection remains a liberatory one, its agency largely conceptualized in terms of resistance to social norms. In a sense, our research has revealed the power implicit in the oft-heard Granola retort, "Huh?" Future research is indicated and will be devoted to observing the effects of the recent importation of tofu and Shittake mushrooms into Granola consumptive practices, social interaction, and self-image.

NOTES:

1. The literature here is copious and weighty. See for example, Spongebob Squarepants (*non de plume*), "Aquatic Culture and the 'Focus on the Family' Phenomenon," *The Journal of Interesting Stuff*, Vol 10, No.3, Spring 2000.

2. Gotmilch, Twinkowitz, and Crunchk, *Playing the Beatles Backwards*. Harvard University Press, 2001.

3. Emeril, Franz. "Granola Power-Avoidance of Sushi Preference and Preferential Treatment," *New York Times*, 7/16/04, section C (food section), p.3.

4. Emeril's radical philosophical platform is predicated on his years of work observing childhood confrontations with parents insistent that their youngsters not go off to school without breakfast.
5. Emeril, section C (food section), p.4.
6. See also (Count) Chochula, Nancy Drew, and Susie Hilton.

* *Bulletin of Sociological Studies*, Vol. 24, No. 2, pp.134-135, 2004.

DOING IT ONLINE

Mark and his buddies, having convinced themselves that the cosmos is filled with aliens and that many of these aliens carry devices with plugs that can be used in either 110, 220, AC, or DC outlets, decided to go into the appliance business. It was either appliances or NASA, but Mark had an extra toe on his right foot and Luke and John had a fear of heights since that bumpy afternoon landing at the fly-in at the Ravalli County Testicle Festival.

Mark and friends were not going to sell just any appliances, but rather appliances aliens would need if they decided to settle down peacefully in Montana, maybe to ranch or maybe not so peacefully to invade human bodies or to perform medical experiments. The All Alien Appliance Co. carried motorized wheel chairs in case aliens did not have feet. There were orange radiation suits in sizes small to extra large. The company invested heavily in battery-chargers, thinking that some aliens would need said equipment to recharge the batteries of their cattle mutilating devices. Mark also bought scuba-diving gear, well aware that aliens might find the pristine air of Montana not to their liking.

However, six months were enough to prove that few aliens were interested, and so in an epiphany of insight the fellows switched to stocking appliances humans would need if aliens carried them off. This was more successful, and Luke then got the idea that since so many Montanans were being transported to distant solar systems, a line of outer space gear and other space travel merchandise should be added to the inventory. And if extra-terrestrials attempted to mate with essential terrestrials to produce a race of quintessential terrestrials or non-essential terrestrials, the All Alien Appliance Co. carried an assortment of contraceptive accouterment unmatched anywhere on the planet.

However, it was All Alien Appliance Co.'s Internet travel service DeepSpace.com that was really the key to success, and reality being what it is, customer emails were overwhelmingly queries about inner space, not outer space, travel. It did not take Small Business Administration information sheets to point out that the merchandising of outer space paraphernalia was a moneymaking field saturated beyond belief. What was needed, however, was a company offering inner space travel advice, maps, clothing, and an endless assortment of contraceptive accouterment.

At first, the fellows got it wrong and thought inner space was the stuff Olama Yanda Ben Contada was up to. How do you sell travel advice and the related trappings for that? But no, "inner space" meant journeys to the center of Earth, or for the only slightly less adventuresome, the bottom of the ocean, or sea, or Lake Superior in the hopes of finding gold bullion from some storm sunk Spanish galleon. Exactly how the Spanish Main included Lake Superior was completely beyond Matt, but travel under the surface of Montana in caves and mine shafts, or to riverbeds and lake bottoms made sense.

"Wasn't the state motto '*Oro y Plata*,' gold and silver?" Matt asked over some Oysters Rockefeller at the Yoinseminateme Alien Café at the rear of All Alien Appliance Co.'s Bozeman store.

"Gold and silver mining," someone offered.

"Spanish, isn't it?"

John, a short fellow with an even shorter memory and therefore absolutely no ability with history or math, joined, "Hey, I'll bet Spanish galleons sailed the seven seas of Canyon Ferry, Holter Lake, Medicine Lake, Fort Peck Lake, and Flathead Lake"

"That's only five."

"Lewis and Clark mapped them?"

"I think these were 1930s CCC projects . . . electrification dam-made lakes."

And then came the all-important, "Well, yes and no."

True, these were manmade lakes of recent construction, "But," said Luke, obviously the deep thinker in the group and therefore always turned to for the final word, "there is absolutely no proof that Spanish galleons did not sail up the Missouri, Yellowstone, and Smith hundreds of years ago, and in the fierce storms that crossed Montana before global weather change, many of those galleons sunk carrying crew and treasure down with them."

"That's right, Juan Pizarro searching for the eight cities of gold," offered mathematician John.

"Seven."

"Six."

"Seven," the issue being settled by a vote.

DeepSpace.com was how Mark met Mary, and that became Montana's most famous romance since Doña Consuela Rodriguez y Sanchez slaughtered her husband's mistresses when she caught the lovely young downstairs maids upstairs. This event was particularly tragic for Don Juan Rodriguez, for all he was doing was attempting to bury his sorrows in the young women. It seems he had just received word that his gold and silver laden keelboats had been sunk in a fierce windstorm that swept across the Missouri River where it joined the Yellowstone. Like Ulysses slaughtering Penelope's untrustworthy maids, Doña Consuela Rodriguez y Sanchez went at Rosa, Miranda, Margarita, and Susanna* with a fury that splattered blood from bed to bath and beyond. Don Juan never recovered from his losses.

In any event Mary's emails to Mark@DeepSpace.com, purportedly about scuba diving Flathead Lake in search of lost Spanish galleons, became friendlier and friendlier until they turned from simply romantic to outright erotic. Maybe Mark should not have taken such a personal interest in Mary's queries, but he chose not to completely overlook the slide from travel questions to erotic travel arrangements.

On a hot August 4, Mary and Mark had torrid sex in a small wooded cove on the northern shore of Flathead Lake. On an equally inflamed August 6, they mated on the west bank of the Yellowstone a couple of miles up from Three Forks near Rick's Sushi Bar. Whether passion knows no bounds, or some bizarre fetish had to be satisfied, they made love in full scuba equipment, rented and serviced by the All Alien Appliance Co. Mask, tank, wet suit, weight belt, and flippers rubbed and writhed on the muddy shore as the lovers consummated their passion. Squeaking and squishing noises rose in the heat of the night air canceling out the cries of ducks and geese, the drone of bees, the buzz of mosquitoes, hum of gnats, whirr of no-see-ums, and the frightful warnings of so many other denizens of the great outdoors.

But unbeknownst to Mary, her fiery passions, sweat and steam, were being sent streaming out of the DeepSpace.com website across the Internet world because Luke, once again demonstrating his intellectual prowess, figured there existed an untapped scuba-fetish market. Love in full scuba gear—heavy breathing underwritten by a tank of air velvet-strapped to one's back, rubber flippers flipping furiously above wet-suit heated fervor, and weight belts banging and banging together—such is the stuff of x-rated, but not illegal, Montana love-making.

All Alien Appliance Co. and DeepSpace.com had found its niche. Daily the website racked up thousands of hits. Emails came in from around the world. Just before All Alien Appliance International stock went public, Mark and his buddies cornered the market in sales of GFCI outlets for lovers who were electrified in dangerously wet areas.

---

* Susanna, the most vivacious and lewd of the downstairs maids, escaped with only minor injuries to her right ear and nose. As Dona Consuela Rodriguez y Sanchez hacked away with her machete, the naked Susanna spun like a toreador and leapt out of the second floor window, landing in the cart full of hay that Pedro had just brought in from one of Don Juan's fields.

Pedro, a young man with a small paw-shaped scar on his forehead received when teaching a wolf to dance, had always loved the raven-haired and bountifully bosomed Susanna, but knowing his master's feelings for her had kept his passion to himself. Seeing her distress, he whipped the cart's oxen team to their speediest best and trundled off down the road. Pedro could not believe his good fortune, and his wooden leg drummed against the cart seat setting up a syncopated rhythm to Susanna's sobs. Neither Doña Consuela Rodriguez y Sanchez nor her husband noticed Pedro's or Susanna's disappearance until the next day, and being exhausted from the previous day's activities and the cleanup that followed, they were in no mood to go after the pair.

Whether out of thankfulness for the deed or simple boredom, Susanna made love to an obviously inexperienced Pedro (he had taken a vow of celibacy in thanks to the Virgin Mary for staunching the blood when his right hand was severed by his brother's sickle as they were harvesting wheat), though for fear of slivers she insisted that he first remove his wooden leg. Mating resulted in Pepito, a strapping young boy who later in life would become a Missouri keelboat captain with a neurotic fear of windstorms. When Pepito was two, Pedro was killed while attempting to teach a bear to dance.

Susanna married Guy St. Côte du Charbonneau, a French fur trapper she met shortly before Pedro died. Susanna could not speak French and Guy 's Spanish vocabulary was limited to "muskrat," "beaver," "buffalo," "whisky," and "sexual intercourse." Whether it was because of some unfathomable compatibility or Guy's habit of leaving pregnant women wherever he traveled, Susanna and Guy produced three children during ten happy years together roaming the upper Northwest in search of pelts.

On June 3, 1787, Guy slipped off a muddy hill that one day would become the site of Havre, Montana, and slid head first into one of his beaver traps. Since the trap was set to spring shut, Guy was immediately decapitated, and Susanna was now left with two children (Philippe and Hernandez had died of some sort of pox). She was taken in by Sammasquat, a Shoshone warrior, and after nine months Susanna presented Sammasquat was a baby girl, Sacajawea.

Unfortunately, at this point Susanna simply vanishes from reality. There are legends, which need not be repeated for few are supported by any evidence whatsoever. One of the silliest claims she was coveted by three old men when she was bathing in a pond. A favorite story, though an unredeemably absurd one, has it that Merriwether Lewis took Susanna back to Tennessee, but whether it was his undaunted courage or her undaunted lasciviousness sometimes aimed at Grinder a tavern owner, or Jacques the wheelwright, or Billy the smithy who worked under a spreading chestnut tree, Lewis was driven to suicide. Except for a pair of French knickers embroidered with a heart and the words "Louie and Sue" that recently turned up on PBS's *Antiques Roadshow*, absolutely nothing can be said for this story. It makes no difference that the owner of the panties, one Mrs. Henrietta Rodgers of New Salem, Tennessee, had heard a story from her father, one passed from great grandfather to grandfather, that the family name had been shortened and anglicized from Rodriguez to Rodgers.

A CASE OF IDENTITY THEFT

Mary Velanucci went to the Glendive rodeo and while she was returning to the stands carrying a hamburger with everything and a second for her daughter, "No mustard, ketchup, pickles, or onions," her wallet slipped from her pocket. When she got home, her first panicked thought was that her wallet had simply vanished—a thought that carried her through to shortly before midnight. After putting her daughter to bed and downing a quiet cup of coffee, she pulled off her jeans, saw the hole, and recalled that the day before she had torn the bottom out of a back pocket when she absent-mindedly jammed in a pair of copper rods after witching for water on her neighbor's ranch.

Mary Velanucci understood who she was by what she carried in her purse and wallet, the bills on her desk, and the papers she kept in a small fireproof box in the attic. The mail order catalogues that deluged her mailbox, hundreds of Victoria's Secrets and L.L. Beans but never a Cabelo's, were especially helpful for defining the parameters of her existence. She did not need Huldah Claire Voyant to find her outer self, the Rastafarians to locate her inner being, nor the Avanda Vey Gavartii Transformers to give her a sense of identity. This was why the Computer Age's scourge, identity theft, was so frightening to her.

Mark Drinkwater found Mary's wallet the next day when he was cleaning up the wrappers, cups, and empty beer cans from under the bleachers. There were two credit cards, VISA and American Express. Next to the five dollars was a crumpled Northwest Power bill. There was also a receipt from Safeway for a loaf of bread, a half-gallon of milk, and a Hershey's candy bar. The picture on her driver's license gave him a good idea of how she looked.

Mark was not always drunk or disreputable, and so he mailed Mary her wallet, and no matter how tempting the five dollars and American Express card were, he left them in place. He dutifully returned her Safeway receipt. But Mark, who was not always drunk and all too frequently disreputable, did not return her driver's license, the VISA card, or the power bill. After years of minimum wage jobs and sleeping at shelters for the homeless or under cardboard and newspapers, Mark Drinkwater was not beyond becoming Mary Veianucci.

Mark did what he did because he could not help it. Mark's father Lukas, failing to make a livelihood first as a circuit preacher (he could never remember the appropriate passages from the Gospels) and then as a Bible salesman, decided on thievery. For a while he was enormously successful, able to support a wife and child, but then one of his convenience store robberies went amiss, and the cashier at the Sweet Grass Gas-n-Go was left bleeding from a bullet in his femur. Lukas, one of the many who try so hard but fail anyway, left his wife and child for twenty years in the state penitentiary.

But Lukas did what he did because he could not help it. He came from a broken family, for Hal and Thecla Drinkwater had broken up over a game of poker. Hal was a sheepherder whose joys in life were singing to his sheep and going into town on a Saturday night to raise hell with his wife, Thecla. One evening Hal was on a winning streak which by ten-thirty had garnered him fifty dollars, a pair of gold-plated cuff links, a leather saddle with a broken stirrup, and two tickets for passage on the Intermountain stage coach from Billings to Helena. His good fortune came to the attention of a barmaid with whom he promptly ran off for two years, leaving Thecla to Paul, a bad poker player but a goodly tent maker who taught her how to sew.

Mark lived as Mary Veianucci and then Mary Van Gates, until he was arrested for bigamy (actually trigamy) and sentenced to join his father for three to five years in prison. With Mary Velanucci's VISA card he bought a blond wig that had a great many curls reaching just past his shoulders. He then visited Belle's Boutique in Billings and bought several dresses, patterned nylons, and two pair of shoes, flats and Italianate high heels. After the VISA card was rejected at the cosmetics counter at Dillard's department store (Mary had called VISA after inspecting the returned wallet), Mark went to a local bank and with driver's license and power bill for identification, opened a checking account with the twenty-two dollars he had put in a can for a rainy day never considering that some day, such as the day Mary Velanucci lost her wallet, would be a sunny one. He explained to the bank clerk that his last name had been misspelled: "'L' does look like 'l' when written in block letters, doesn't IT to everyone living in IllINOIS?"

Back at Dillard's, he spent considerable time trying to decide if Mary looked more like a Clinque woman or Susie Hilton. Settling on Hilton, he bought just the right shade of lipstick, powder, foundation, and lash-enhancer. He visited the lingerie department and then the faux jewelry counter. Shopping bags full, he rushed to the restroom at the Exxon Service station just off I-90 at the 27th street underpass, where for thirty minutes to the yells of several female customers and finally the service station cashier, he worked to become Mary Veianucci. In fact, he became more beautiful than the original Mary ever was or will be.

There was the blond hair set with beads for a "perfect 10" dazzling appearance. There was the make-up that brought out his eyes and gave his lips an alluring pout. The dress was one of those Chinese affairs, form-fitting and up to the neck, in red and blue satins and dragons and lotus flowers. Since Mark never had much beard, the cosmetic foundation hid what there was and the high neck on the dress hid scattered chest hairs. The push-up bra stuffed with the teenager's fix, Scott tissue, gave him and the dress an appealing bust, and the high heels produced a well-turned derriere. Mark liked it, and as he left the restroom, a humble gasp issued from the men waiting at the cash register.

If Mark/Mary had limited himself/herself to passing bad checks, his/her life might have gone its merry way. If Mark/Mary had limited himself/herself to marketing Mary Kaye cosmetics (he won a pink Cadillac for selling thousands of dollars of the stuff), his/her life might have safely continued on its happy path. If Mark/Mary had limited himself/herself to dating wealthy CEOs who had recently retired and moved to Montana ranchettes, all might have gone well. But he/she and Seattle's Wilhelm Van Gates, who was getting a hair replacement and tummy tuck at the Big Mountains Sky Resort Clinic just outside of Big Mountains, fell in love.

Of course, it was not long before Van Gates found out that Mark/Mary was considerably more Mark than Mary, but Van Gates did not mind. As Van Gates put it, "Thirty-five years I was married to a woman; isn't that enough?" And Mark did make a wonderful woman: his make-up was expertly applied; he walked confidently in three-and-a-half-inch heels; and he had an assortment of costumes that could turn him from an innocent girl scout to a tempting cheerleader to a sultry chanteuse to a nasty whore as the occasion demanded. And all this without the need for any sort of sex change operation.

They were married in a lavish ceremony at Van Gates' ranchette, which overlooked Flathead Lake. Friends came, as did the paparazzi, and photos turned up in *Vanity Fare* and *The Upper Crust*, and so many Internet sites. Mark was titled "the mystery bride," his unknown origins enabling comparisons to Eliza Doolittle. He was described with such adjectives as "beautiful," "stunning," "sensual," and "exotic," and within weeks fashion designers were taking their cue from Mark's wedding trousseau. A short while later Wal-Mart, Kmart, and Target had their designers fashioning cheap knock-offs for the world's poor.

It was only after Louise, a secretary deep in the Montana Department of Records, discovered upon filing the marriage certificate that one Mary Velanucci ("'L' does look like 'l' when written in block letters, doesn't IT to everyone living in IllINOIS?") was already married to a fellow named Lampwick that Mark/Mary's dream life came to an end. Since this was only a small secretarial error, the error needed to be compounded by other state employees who took the matter under their purview, and the police and a coterie of immensely moral social workers were at Mary Velanucci's door terrifying mother and daughter. Mary explained with paper certification produced from her small fireproof box in the attic that, "Yes," she had been married to Jonathan Lampwick, and "Yes" he was the father of her daughter, but she was not the wife of a second husband named "Mark" whether at the same time or serially with Jonathan.

"Could this simply be a case of clerical error?" Mary suggested.

The room went quiet until in an eerie unison her visitors announced that the State of Montana does not make clerical errors. "No, nope, never," and then they sat down again on the couch.

Maybe it was the shock of the icy retort, but it brought Mary to recall the missing wallet of two years before. She told her story, ending with a dreaded, "Could this be a case of identity theft?"

To that everyone said, "Now that's possible, likely, yes, of course," and when the State of Montana's upholders of law and order had retired to a sushi bar they had recently heard good things about, they concluded over cleverly arranged bits of raw fish that Mary Veianucci's marriage certificate was the spawn of identity theft. Sometime during lunch, the report was stamped with a smiley face and a Post-It sticky note that read, "Identity theft . . . investigate further."

Back at the Montana Department of Records an official who recently had been promoted from a cubicle to an office read the file, spilled cream and coffee on the words "Identity theft" and sent it back to Louise who seeing only the "investigate further," routed it to someone with an impressive badge and therefore could do amazing things to the citizens of Montana. Purely by coincidence, but reality does that sometimes, said badge-carrier was working on the paternity case of one Maria Valdez who had married Jake Veiannucci in 1997 and since no divorce decree was to be found in the files, the badge-bearer smirked and thought, "Could Maria Veiannucci be a bigamous Mary Velanucci?" This supposition, of course, was completely wrong, but so what? And then, someone who had renewed an expired driver's license for one Mary Veianucci and was having a beer with the badge-carrier who had conjured up the bigamy, mentioned that a very attractively dressed Mary, who looked just like Paris Hilton, had given as a reference a man she said was her husband, one Mark Drinkwater. Another smirk and "Of course, this ain't the first case of polyandry we've come 'cross in Montana."

Mark/Mary's, Drinkwater/ Veianucci's dream life came to an end. Arrested, charged, found guilty, he was sentenced to the women's facility at Deer Lodge penitentiary. Though he was able to retain his blond wig, the beads had to go as he might use them in a suicide attempt. Sadly, he had to return the pink Cadillac to Mary Kay cosmetics, but happily he got to know his father as a loving and kind inmate.

Without Canadian Club or Four Roses or much chance for larceny, Mark lost his traditional disreputability and became a model prisoner. The warden, noting prisoner Mary's talents, asked that she teach cosmetology classes in the prison's rehabilitation program. Coming to the aid of some of the more attractive female prisoners, Mary occasionally went back to being Mark, and so things were not so bad after all. Mark earned his GED, learned the art of Bible salesmanship from his father, and faithfully kept to a low carb diet. After being discharged in eighteen months for good behavior, Mark vanished. Simply vanished.

FIGHTING THE GOOD FIGHT

In an old mining camp somewhere outside of Logan, Montana, a cabal of scientists churns out a constant stream of literature aimed at destroying Christianity. They labor night and day, in the sweat of summer, when the snow on the roof makes the rafters creak, when the spring rains drip through ceilings and file cabinets and computers must be kept under tarpaulins and yards of black PVC. Electricity comes from a large gas-powered generator and if that breaks down, a second in the same ramshackle barn instantly takes over so that the work can go on without interruption.

The main cabin, maybe fifteen feet by twenty, has a long covered corridor running out of a side wall to a second cabin and then to a third and fourth. It is a spider's web of a compound, hidden by trees from any sort of aerial detection. When the scientists are not hard at work at the banks of computers or in the labs, they hold classes for preachers and Sunday school teachers, so these shepherds of the flock can go back to their pastures to infect the sheep with doubt as to the soundness of Sts. Peter and Paul's religion.

Before the intense research of a small coterie of mainline ministers, code-named "The Saviors," no one knew exactly where the mining camp was located. People had only a suspicion that it was somewhere in the Beartooth Mountains, which meant anywhere within thousands of square miles of dense forest. Not even the scientists who worked there knew the location. Like pony express riders, drivers of transport SUVs would only cover part of the distance from Bozeman to the compound. One driver meets a scientist at the Bozeman Airport. This driver takes his charge to the Logan Trailways Bus Depot. There, a second driver, back-tracking, takes his charge in a Suburu up Montana 85, a small paved road that soon turns to gravel on its way to the village of Menard. Here the passenger is transferred to a Ford Explorer that works its way farther north to Maudlow just at the edge of the Gallatin National Forest. Then a Hummer equipped with tow chains and winch leaves the gravel road somewhere short of Ringling and winds its way deep into the Bridger range on a rough two-track. Finally, the scientist is met by men with AK47s, one of the finest assault rifles ever made, and escorted on horseback to an amalgam of cabins, bunkhouse, barn, several sheds, and garage. The compound has only one entrance, a path six feet wide through coils of barbed wire and randomly buried claymore landmines.

Once inside the compound, scientists and others can work at the banks of computers to prove that macro-evolution never occurred, at telescopes searching for evidence that the universe is only six thousand years old, and in laboratories designed to disprove carbon-dating. But the real work, the labor that requires the especial "High Colonic Clearance" goes on deep beneath the toilet floor. The commode swings up, boards slide away, and a deep hole is revealed. A long aluminum ladder descends to a platform at ten feet, then a second ladder drops to twenty feet and finally a third reaches to a horizontal tunnel at thirty feet. This old mine shaft winds to a complex of bunkers that have been floored with chip-seal technology, painted in Indo-Flack mauve, and concrete-reinforced to withstand a thermonuclear attack in the range of 40 kiloton. It is here that only those special few with High Colonic Clearance, the inner circle, the dedicated to the death cadre, sworn to a blood-oath of "each according to its own kind," are to be found.*

The Saviors knew that what transpired in such a place was nothing less than the destruction of Christianity. Atheist scientists, parading as Bible-literalist Creation Scientists, were at work turning the Holy Scriptures into an elementary school science textbook. Atheist scientists pretending to be god-fearing Christians were toiling to turn Genesis' creation story into astronomy, astrophysics, biology, and zoology, Noah's flood into geology and hydrology, and the Tower of Babel into anthropology. Atheist scientists were transmuting Chronicles into history books and Ezekiel into a space-travel manual. The Gospels were to be twisted into psychology texts rivaling the weighty insights found in *Reader's Digest* and *Parade Magazine*. Atheist sociologists spun St. Paul's letters into social documents promoting divorce, and worse, the termination of humanity through the advocacy of celibacy.

The Saviors knew that atheist Creation Scientists—like Communist *aparachik*s or terrorists, well-organized, dedicated, and as devious as any Lenin, Stalin, or Osama Bin Laden—have spent the last half century at this Montana retreat in a devilish attempt to transform abiding faith, faith that gives meaning and sustenance to difficult lives, into dull fact. This fifth column for the forces of atheism was pillaging Jewish and Christian scriptures—God's divine word as revealed in the hearts and minds of prophets, rabbis, apostles, and a host of latter-day knights-errant—to serve their one perverse desire: to demean, debase, and ultimately destroy the Christian faith.

---

* The final team of construction workers and the architect who designed this bunker were killed when the four Huey helicopters they were riding in crashed just outside of Bozeman. The cause of the crash remains unexplained.

The Saviors knew that the conspirators, blind to any understanding of God's creation except through the white cane of science, wanted to replace the Good News with the Gospel of Creation Science. This was truly seeing reality through a glass darkly. These Bible-destroyers aspired to nothing less than the annihilation of every gift to humanity given by God: the ability to reason, the ability to distinguish the sacred from the profane, the ability to turn hate into love. Creationists also understood that they were building a radical political ideology and so the "ism" at the end of "Creationism" is apt.

Knowing the enemy did not come easy. Maybe the Saviors made far too many mistakes and took too many missteps. They had a mission but never bothered to write up a mission statement. They forgot to frame a list of objectives and had no planning document that they could revise in lengthy meetings every other year. Where were the power-point lectures and the breakout sessions? When a decision had to be made, they actually voted instead of reaching a consensus. Yet their quest continued, and when the Creation Science agenda was fully grasped, the compound's location finally discovered, and the leaders identified, a plan of attack could be devised and put into action.

Just to locate the compound took the Saviors twenty years. Its secret existence, rumored since 1984, was finally confirmed by a close inspection of page seventy-eight of Dan Brown's *Da Vinci Code* read while playing the Beatles' "Let It Be" backwards at seventy-eight rpm. In several instances, fathers passed on to their daughters and sons the task when they became too old to carry on (or too scared after Louis Leverage was found hanging from an oak and Martha Teebine was hit by Saint Paul Freebolt's tractor on Christmas day.)

And unspoken by the Saviors, deep within each soul, the questions haunted, "Why haven't Christians awoken to this debasement?" "Why are they not only duped but also participants in this destruction of their faith?" "Where is the sense in all this . . . the logic . . . must reality really be this strange?" Maybe the answer was so obvious that it did not need saying. Who does not know that newspaper reporters, magazine essayists, and television news anchors are left-wing, secular humanist, evolutionary throwback, pinko-intellectual atheists who would be happy to see Christianity destroyed. The last thing such miscreants as these would want is to expose Creation Scientists for what they really are—Satan's chaplains.

Louis Leverage Jr. worked closely with several foreign dignitaries from Pakistan, North Korea, and Iran to secure a backpack nuclear weapon of small yield, about a half kiloton. The nuclear device was activated when a Tampax containing a nine-volt battery was slid into a plastic water bottle Velcro-strapped to the side of the backpack. Fitted with a detonator and a timing device that had been stolen from an old James Bond movie set, the bottle was connected to the bomb by copper wires that ran through the backpack's left and right shoulder straps. Marla Teebine and Mary Mapledrop were to enter the compound disguised as South Dakota Creationists who carried documents that proved the identity of the Intelligent Designer once and for all. After entering the compound, they were to ask to use the bathroom where they would slide back the flooring, insert the Tampax in the water bottle to activate the detonator, and then drop it and the backpack bomb down the entrance hole to the subterranean bunker. Given the chip-seal technology, the Indo-Flack mauve, and concrete reinforcement, only a blast from within could destroy the compound's nerve center.

On May 12, Marla and Mary signed the guest book. Their passes and papers were checked and re-checked—passes and papers they had secured from a man who had the inner circle, sworn to the blood-oath of "each according to its own kind," High Colonic Clearance. Barely a year before, Marla and Mary had pretended to be seduced by a Creation Scientist at a church potluck in Hardin, after which, sperm sample in hand, they threatened to expose his misdeed. They finally got the needed documents nine months later when they emailed the mark that they would blog to the world that he had forced them to undergo abortions in a Tijuana backroom in the third trimester of their respective pregnancies.

Someone exceptionally short in a white lab coat seated Marla and Mary at a computer terminal. Ostensibly researching politicians who were attempting to foist Intelligent Design arguments and equal treatment for equal theories on school boards, biology teachers, and home schoolers, the two Saviors pretended to take notes, compile lists, and download pictures. Knowing what they were going to do next, they were tense and twice clicked the mouse's right button instead of the left.

At 1:45 Marla and Mary requested permission to use the bathroom. They closed the document they were viewing and shut their notebooks. All looked good, but somehow in their nervousness they knocked the water bottle detonator from the backpack nuclear weapon's Velcro-strip, and the detonator hit the floor with a clatter sufficient to draw the attention of the several guards in the room. Someone sounded the alarm bell, red lights flashed, and Marla and Mary went racing down a long corridor toward the next cabin and the bathroom.

Mary never made it; she was shot dead as she passed the hall monitor just outside the floor director's office. The bullet entered her side between the third and fourth ribs and cut into her right lung and then her heart, which deflected it northward through the ascending aorta to her throat paralleling the path of the carotid artery. The slug came to a rest in her brain, anterior lobe. Though such damage should have meant instantaneous death, Mary miraculously remained conscious long enough to unstrap the backpack, hand it over at a run to Marla, and sing out the entire twenty-third psalm. Holding the backpack before her, Marla kept on, weaving from side to side just missing a torrent of bullets. Turning off the global positioning device hidden in the stem of her eyeglasses, she ran on intuition toward the bathroom, swung through the doorway, lifted a board, and as if some great cosmic force was with her, she dropped the backpack and water bottle with precision through the hole.

Marla did not stop to look at her success. She cartwheeled through the bathroom window as a bullet glanced off her right ear. She ran to the compound's entrance, screaming at a stunned guard, and then less than a hundred yards from the last coil of barbed-wire, Marla felt the earth beneath her tremble, shake, and heave. The backpack had done its job.

For how long she ran she did not know, but if she had cared to stop and listen, she would have known that no one was following her for the entire mining camp had caved in and those who were still alive could only tiptoe through the claymores. She buckled twenty-six minutes later in a clearing seven miles from the compound, and so like the incredible few before her, she had broken the unbreakable four-minute mile. Heart straining against a 36C brassiere, Marla was picked up by a small helicopter that came out of nowhere and brought safely back to the Abyssinian Baptist Full Gospel Church in Bozeman. To those gathered around her, she said, "It is finished," and collapsed.

The Saviors know that atheist Creation Scientists—like Communist *aparachik*s or terrorists, well-organized, dedicated, and as devious as any Lenin, Stalin, or Osama Bin Laden—have spent the last half century in a sordid attempt to turn abiding faith, faith that gives meaning and sustenance to difficult lives, into dull fact. The Saviors are America's last bulwark against atheism, and they will fight Creation Scientists wherever Satan's minions set up shop.

LIVING ON THE EDGE OF LIFE

Where can you go after growing up in Butte's Meaderville or a few miles away in Anaconda in the 1950s? Except for extractive industries and smelters, it is all ramshackle bungalow filled with second generation Polish, and Irish, Welsh, Swedes, Italians (long "i"), and a few Germans. Down the block on Mercury Street was the Workers of the World office just around the corner from the Polka Dot Polka Club. Every other garage had a polka band practicing, or maybe just a couple of people with accordions and some kind of horn.

This is the land of things are a hell of a lot better when the mines are choked with dynamite dust and the smelters are coating the landscape with soot. This is the era of the Korean War, black listing, Eisenhower playing golf, drive-in movies, and McDonalds with fewer than 100,000 hamburgers sold. The times demand rented tuxedos for weddings and taffeta prom dresses and the invention of juvenile delinquents.

Children of the '50s found the threat of the creature from the black lagoon, triphids, and giant tarantulas as frightening as A bombs and H. *I Led Three Lives, The Honeymooners, Westinghouse Theatre, Your Show of Shows,* and Uncle Milty were on the black and white televisions whose reception improved by redirecting the rabbit ears and could be fixed by giving the cabinet a good whack. Of course, if you did not own a TV, the set in the front window of Lukovich's Television and Appliance Store was on just so you could watch the Friday Night Fights brought to you by Pabst Blue Ribbon.

In 1957 two things happened that changed the world, except for Butte, forever. The Soviet Union sent a dog into space, and thousands of people across the United States were abducted by Martians who came to Earth solely for the purpose of rounding up humans so that they could be transmuted into mindless robots of the most terrifying sort. None of this would have been reported in Montana newspapers if the Soviet satellite had not been sending out a constant beeping signal and every single American except for those abducted by Martians had not been worried about the fate of the dog the Russian spacecraft had carried. Bolshevist dog-murderers were proving once more how heartless a Commie could be.

The year Butte changed forever was 1980. The Big Pit, the Berkeley Pit, began shutting down its mining operations; the smelters in Anaconda soon followed; and, the point of this time-travelogue becomes clear.

Though kept secret for decades by the U.S. government, newly released documents through the Freedom of Information Act detail how the thousands of Americans who had been carried off in flying saucers were returned to the United States reconfigured as completely mindless, spineless, and soulless liberals. As to why our government thought that this liberal invasion had to be kept secret until it commissioned Rush Limbaugh to reveal it, who knows? But by the 1980s, Rush Limbaugh, and Jerry Falwell, and Pat Robertson, and Ronald Reagan (after being briefed by Nancy) were on to the Martians' game plan.

The Martians had returned thousands of "abductees" as liberals programmed to undermine the moral, social, and religious fabric of American life. Aliens had hardwired these liberals with arguments promoting evolution, atheism, environmentalism, fluoridated water, sexual equality, affirmative action plans, and a vast variety of entitlement programs. It soon became apparent to talk show radio hosts that liberals across the nation were promoting the virtues of homosexuality, fighting to remove prayer and Christmas pageants from public schools, and wrenching the Ten Commandments and Christmas crèches from courthouses. Liberals were praising international peace initiatives instead of dying to defend America. And all this was going on while millions of unborn babies formerly known as fetuses were being murdered by unwed female liberals whose indiscriminate sex with any male but especially men who had taken illegal drugs at Club 54 had led to unplanned pregnancies. Then there were the unwed mothers who had taken a vow of celibacy until marriage, but after being brutally raped by liberal males were duped by liberal physicians into aborting their babies eleven weeks into the last trimester.

The swarm of liberals that the Martians secreted in Montana (they had first been stationed in California) demanded that lumberjacks should be retrained as motel housekeepers so that the spotted owls up at Columbia Falls could rest easy that their native habitat was secure. Liberals also were occupied with reintroducing wolves and saving trout from whirling disease while hunters and snowmobilers were being shut out of their chance to enjoy the winter wonders of Yellowstone Park.

And in Butte the word got out that liberals were behind the closing of the Big Pit, the Berkeley Pit. A cabal of liberals, because it would take more than any single or even a couple of liberals to close a mining operation that had successfully leveled an entire mountain, secreted in New York, Chicago, and San Francisco had done it. Then when the smokestacks of the Anaconda smelters stopped spewing their colorful volumes of ash, soot, and smoke, it was hard times and no one could doubt that liberals were behind that, too. The sad truth was that liberals were more interested in keeping Montana's rivers, streams, and children free from pollutants than giving miners a hole to dig in.

Where can you go after growing up in Butte's Meaderville or a few miles away in Anaconda in the 1950s? Here you are in 2005, your heroes are dead, an era has passed, and you are pushing 50, out of work, out of beer, time on your hands, with nothing to do but to listen to the jerks on talk radio. Your offspring have joined the Marines. Your wife has left for the city lights of Helena, Missoula, Billings, or Bozeman. A few years ago in a big tent you became a Real Christian but that did not help. You could become a Christian missionary to Zimbabwe, but you are not sure that even the Zimbabweians want you. The only thing of which you can be certain is that worse than the Commies are the liberals, who like some body-snatching invasion and it-came from-outer-space crop-circle-cutting cattle mutilators have destroyed Butte and Meaderville and Anaconda, and if not stopped, everyone's hometown is next.

GREAT FALLS SPACE PORT

Senators Max Burns and Conrad Baucus have made it possible for Montana to receive more tax dollars back from the U.S. government than Montanans send in. This goes a long way in keeping Montana in existence, for without such largess not the entire state but two-thirds would vanish from the map of North America. Some agribusiness would still exist; Paradise Valley where live so many Hollywood stars would continue to flourish as would white water rafting, hunting, and trout fishing; The Thong Corporation, Yellowstone Added Value Industries, and Job Indo-European Cell Phone Stem Cell Fuel Cells Transnational, Inc. would go on; and, of course there will always be Indian reservations. But Butte would disappear as would Two Dot and Three Forks; Sweet Grass and Big Timber; Bearmouth, Cutbank, Reedpoint, Geyser, Polson and Powderville; Lodge Pole, Deer Lodge, Red Lodge, Lodge Grass; and so many others.

Some of the returned tax dollars upkeep the Montana National Guard, which is important since there are Montanans worried about the recent invasion of Californians and New Yorkers. Some of the monies go to the War on Drugs. Some keep the interstate highway system intact. Some of the monies teamed with local funds support specialty programs like weather stations, chip seal research, and suicide prevention education.

So, there was great concern throughout Montana when the Cold War came to an end with the end of the Cold War. A few miles outside of Great Falls were the most wondrous contrivances of human invention, missile silos which contained nuclear armed missiles aimed each and every one at each and every person in the USSR. If these were not needed anymore, a lot of people would find themselves without their federal paychecks. It was not only the fellows down in the silos whose fingers hovered above the button who would be jobless, but also caterers, grounds keepers, cable guys, and a host of bartenders and exotic dancer in Great Falls, itself.

It will probably never be settled whether the local Democratic or Republican organizations, the Chamber of Commerce, or the Lady's Auxiliary of the Church of Peace and Love suggested using the silos as the key element in the Great Falls Inter-Cosmological Space Port, but it was a brilliant if seemingly absurd idea. Florida has Cape Canaveral, Texas has the Houston Control Center, and so what's wrong with Montana? The state certainly was good enough for intercontinental ballistic missiles. Then someone suggested that they knew of a hometown boy who had studied cosmology, one Matthew Lunes, and at present being unemployed, he was free to direct the project.

Not against all odds, Senators Baucus and Burns were able to bring home the bacon. It seems that President Bush needed their two votes to secure the necessary funding for a war with Greenland which intelligence gathered by the CIA demonstrated with singular certainty had been stockpiling weapons of mass destruction since the 1830s. Of more recent date Greenlanders had been smuggling explosives in old Viking raiding boats and then deploying dynamite laden whales up and down the east coast of the United States, ready to be washed aground at a moment's notice. In return for their votes, Baucus and Burns' Great Falls Inter-Cosmological Space Port was the recipient of seed money to the sum of a half billion dollars.

It was as if the Music Man himself had come to town. Committees of various sorts were assembled; there were break-out sessions, focus groups, and lots of two by three foot paper sheets taped up with everyone's suggestions on them. A flow chart was devised, and objects, goals, and timelines were determined. Local churches offered up prayers of thanksgiving for Matthew Lunes who realized not a minute too soon that the whole adventure was about to come to naught, because no one had remembered to write up a mission statement.

And so, on April 1, 2005, completed right on time, except for the plumbing and some wiring for the lighting, the Great Falls Inter-Cosmological Space Port came into existence, and it would have worked fine if only NASA had any use for it. The Space Port was very pretty, all done up in Indo-Flack mauve concrete, iron-red beams, several nice guardhouses, a self-service restaurant and a gourmet cafe that featured Kobi beef. There were satellite dishes and radio telescopes all over the place, and nearly eighteen hundred computer terminals. The Literature Department at the University of Great Falls, using such phrasing as "core deployment motivation," "fractional adjustment assessment," and "localizable resource management allocator," had fashioned completely undecipherable instruction manuals for maintenance crews and operations personnel. But to quote an exasperated Matthew Lunes six months after the ribbon was cut, "Hey, we ain't got no business." Aliens might be making crop circles over at the Hendersons' place, or absconding with tourists in Yellowstone Park, but they certainly were not refueling or anything else at the Great Falls Inter-Cosmological Space Port. People were getting angry and then the whispering started that they should have used the silos for a sort of Nuclear War theme park with rides and so on.

Unlike a neat, tidy short story or novel, reality can begin anywhere it chooses, then wander off only to show up later somewhere else as somewhat familiar while somehow different. Reality can appear out of nowhere for no reason at all and it can end not by ending but by simply fading out. Destinations are not reached, the signposts do not point, and it is all a jumble of highways and byways, roadways and crossroads, side streets and alleys, trail, track, and path.

Well, since reality works as it will, but logic always sticks to the straight path, Tibet decided to become a democracy, and that meant that the country's dictator would have to go. The problem was the Tibetans were quite poor as their leader had secreted millions in foreign aid in a Swiss bank, and so they could not afford a really good assassin. Then they saw the ad for the Great Falls Inter-Cosmological Space Port in the *Great Falls Tribune*.

It seems Lunes had heard from a friend who heard from a friend that years before the Thong Corporation over in Billings had had working for it a truly gifted advertising executive, Miriam Rosen, who wrote advertising copy that could sell anything. In fact, she was a key player in turning Thong into a multi-million dollar enterprise. Googling the name, then hiring a detective agency, and finally consulting Huldah Claire Voyant who said look near a pond or lake or roadway by a stand of trees or line of bushes either outdoors or in a garage, Lunes located Miriam Goldstein nee Rosen and with great persuasion installed her as Director of Public Relations. Her first promotional advertisement was sensational. It featured a cut from *Stars Wars III: The Curse of Rummy* with the caption: "Cut rate prices on any launch from the Great Falls Inter-Cosmological Space Port. Bring your own rocket or use one of ours!" To date the Great Falls Inter-Cosmological Space Port has launched into orbit or beyond eight deposed dictators, five generals convicted of war crimes, three televangelists, and two deceased icons.

As its fame spread, Great Falls found itself in a building boom, with high rise condominiums obscuring stunning views of the Rocky Mountains. Hiltons and Sheratons were edging out the Best Western and Holiday Inn Express as all sorts of government leaders came searching for solutions to their problems. The Motel 6 survived the gentrification only because small-time revolutionaries and guerrilla fighters could not afford better. Telecommunications could bank on Job Indo-European Cell Phone Stem Cell Fuels Cells Transnational, Inc. to provide the necessary high-tech support. Even the food court at the High Plains Shopping Mall saw an increase in the amount of Chinese and Mexican food it sold, while Tibetan and Iranian food stalls opened their doors.

All the people from all over Montana who had been put out of work by liberals bent on shutting down open pit mines, stopping logging deforestation, and ending smokestack industry water pollution, flocked to the huge job market opening up in Great Falls. Unemployed miners from Butte, lumbermen from Whitefish, asbestos workers from Libby, and aluminum plant laborers from Columbia converged on the high paying jobs in Great Falls. Miners became maitre d's, lumbermen were now hotel concierges, and factory workers ran antique shops, art galleries, and lingerie boutiques.

Life was fine and Matthew Lunes found himself thinking of running for President of the United States. Miriam Rosen suggested the catchy campaign slogan, "If it's good for Montana, you betcha it's good for the United States!"

RIDE AN OLD PAINT

Old Bill Jones came to Montana to corral the used car market. He had read somewhere that most Montanans are not particularly well-to-do, so he figured that they buy used cars rather than new. His reasoning was not altogether incorrect, so after many years of hard work, his venture met with success. Old Bill had not always been old; it was just what he had been called for as long as anyone could remember. Because his father, William Jones, had named him William Jr. and because his mother had named William Jr.'s younger brother Bill after her father, he was forever after called Old Bill and the second Bill was called Baby Bill.

Old Bill drove an '79 Honda Prelude, not a car of which to be proud, but it got him where he was going as long as he did not need to go there too fast. After the rust began showing through, he hand painted its right front fender and hood and called the car Old Paint. Because the car burned oil and somewhere in the exhaust there was a leak, he did not mind that his window did not roll up all the way, though blowing winter snows could be troublesome. He smelled of oil and gasoline when he was rounding up clunkers, but when he sold them, he wore his good suit and smelled of Ralph Lauren Cowboy Cologne.

To round up cars for his used car lot, he did not visit the Missoula auction house, thinking he knew better how to get better deals on better cars. He visited outback ranches, farms, looked for junkers in coulees, and beaters in the draws. He would load the "little doggies," as he called them, onto his trailer, old Dan. He employed a genius high school dropout mechanic to smooth out transmissions, unstick valves and carburetors, and get another twenty thousand or so out of once fiery motors. He hired a couple of body men, Harry and his lover Harvey, who could straighten dents, work out Montana-sized hail pings, clean up upholstery, and get the radios to work again.

Bill was a happy sort of fellow—happiest when he was selling cars. His used car lot in Billings was followed by a second in Helena, then one in Butte, and a fourth in Missoula. The paradigm car salesman, his face was set in a perfect "I'm a sucker for a deal that will lose me money." He shook every hand, and knew every Montana college and high school coach, captain, quarterback, and team score. He was a Rotarian, Mason, a member of every Chamber of Commerce, and a devout parishioner at just short of two-dozen Christian churches. His cars came with a three-month money back guarantee and a free oil change or tire rotation for the first year. His car lots were festooned with balloons and on Saturdays smelled of hot dogs and chili. Every so often he would put out an old steamer trunk he had painted up with glitter as his "treasure chest" and have a drawing for a free trip for two to Hawaii or the Caribbean. His television spots showed him waving his John Deere cap as he yelled, "Tails matted from too many hours in that tractor seat? Back all raw from sittin' in that harvester? Now's the time get yourself over to Old Bill's Like-New Used Cars!"

Old Bill struck the mother lode when he discovered how much money was to be made in the import-export business. To a man, recent New York, Los Angeles, and Chicago transplants wanted to be the Montanans they had seen on The History Channel or in the pages of *National Geographic*s and so had to drive Lexus, BMW, and Mercedes SUVs or Suburus except during football season when for tailgate parties they had to have rusty Ford 150s, dented Jimmies, and Silverado clunkers, all fitted out with a couple of big dogs, over-sized tires, air freshener dangling from the mirror, and rifle rack. So Old Bill bought their Lexus, BMWs, and Mercedes sedans, which he exported nation-wide over Ebay and then imported brand new Lexus, BMWs, and Mercedes SUVs. As for the Ford 150s, Jimmies, and Silverado clunkers, those were harder to come by, but he did his best. It was at this time that he changed his line to a more refined, "Everyone motors at Old Bill's Automotive Luxury Superstore."

Old Bill's daughter Marie went to the University of Montana. She studied accounting, economics, and business administration. She was a straight A student. An exceptionally beautiful young woman, she decided to have sex one Saturday night and though the fellow was courteous, kind, obedient, cheerful, and passably handsome, she never got his name and really did not enjoy much of it, and so she would be forty-six before trying sex again.

Bill's wife was killed in a poolroom brawl in Black Sulphur Springs. She had made a fortune, lost it, and made another as a pool hall hustler. Mary Elvira Sue Ellen, though it was sometimes Sue Ellen, or Mary Elvira Ellen, or Merry Quitecontraree, looked like the velvet painting that hung in the Butte Miners Saloon. In fact Old Bill had met her in the Butte Miners Saloon where she had an attractive way of racking up balls that brought her skirt to expose just about an inch of her black velvet panties. That day her hair was velvet black, though by fall she wore it red which stayed that way until after the week spent in the Silver Bow county jail when she dyed it blond.

Old Bill's son Mark took after Old Bill's wife. He went wrong. He got into the business of bringing drugs in from Canada; not illegal drugs, but legal drugs that were cheaper purchased in Calgary than in Choteau. The FBI stopped him just south of Polson after he bumped over the Montana Rail Link railroad crossing and the trunk floor dropped out of one of his father's used cars.

Old Bill died the way he lived, riding all over Montana throwing the hoolihan over cars he knew would sell, resell, and resell again before they expired. By the time of his untimely death, he had cornered the Montana used car, new car, SUV, and pickup truck markets. In fact he was voted "Businessman of the Year" in 1996, 1999, and posthumously in 2003. Still raring to go, he died in a crash, his life ended when he hit three large boulders that had tumbled onto US 2 just outside Glacier Park.

Old Bill was given the funeral he deserved and would have wanted. Marie tied his corpse to the rotting bucket seat behind the steering wheel of his Honda Prelude. He and Old Paint were towed on Old Dan to the broad flat plains of eastern Montana and with the gas pedal wedged a quarter way down he was sent off heading west, riding across the prairie that he loved best in search of that junkyard in the sky. They say down at the many car lots that he left behind that whenever you hear rumbling across the big skies of the Big Sky country that's Old Bill starting up another clunker.

Marie took over the business in 2002 after the judge made it clear that Mark would not be out of prison before 2015. A woman who did not have to manage a husband, Marie would turn Old Bill's Automotive Luxury Superstore into a subsidiary of her Land Transportation Unlimited, the international conglomerate that today controls fully two-thirds of all the moving van, refrigerator truck, eighteen wheeler, pickup, passenger automobile, bus, streetcar, taxicab, rickshaw, jitney, and hovercraft rentals worldwide.

You betcha Old Bill is still singing from morning till night.

AN OLD MONTANA SONG

"I ride an old paint, I lead an old dan, I am going to Montana to throw the hoolihan. They feed in the coulees, and they water in the draw. Their tails are all matted, and their backs are all raw.

"Ride around little doggies, ride around them slow, for the fiery and snuffy are raring to go.

"Old Bill Jones had a daughter and a son. One went to college, the other went wrong. His wife, she was killed in a pool-hall fight, but still he sings from morning till night.

"When I die take my saddle from the wall, place it on my old pony, and lead him, out of his stall. Tie my bones to my saddle and turn our faces to the west, and we will ride the prairie we love best."

AND ANOTHER

"I come from Montana, I wear a bandanna. My spurs are all silver, my pony is gray. While riding the ranges, my luck never changes. With foot in the stirrup, I gallop away."

POST SCRIPT

On February 20, 2005, the twentieth century came to an end. Let it be the long century. On the other hand, if as many historians claim, the twentieth century did not begin till 1914 when either a madman or a patriot thought to assassinate Archduke Ferdinand in Sarajevo, the twentieth century comes up nine years short. Then there is the fact that everyone celebrated the century's turn on January 1, 2000, while every chronologist was saying to no one listening that they had to wait to 2001. The bickering can stop now: on February 20, 2005, the twentieth century came to end.

Matt, two buttons to the south on his silk Armani shirt, and Martha, naked and vegan, were doing some veggie burgers in the microwave when the news came over NPR. Across town Mark and Mary were out walking with Corky and Sax, their beautifully matched pair of golden Labs, one six the other five, when they heard the screams coming from neighbors' houses. Moses Goldstein was stacking his last cord of wood for the winter, when he got the phone call. Pastor Bill had just finished working at safe sex with someone he met the night before at the Great God Almighty Invincible singles' dance. When Huldah Claire Voyant was told, all she could say was, "I knew it a month ago." It was like this all over Montana; an era came to an end, and frightened people were crying, "How will common sense and luck light the way now?"

Unlike most other states in the Union, Montana has breathable air. Streets are not littered with trash. Sidewalks are passable because the shopping cart homeless, bag ladies, doorway squatters, and refuse-can poachers prefer the heat of the Miami swamp and the handout flow of the New York matrix. A state two-thirds the size of France, its population remains far short of a million. Nevertheless, as unique as Montana might be, it is completely up to date with telecommunications, multiplex cinema showing first-run movies, and mega-malls, so only those who have dedicated their lives to not knowing could have not heard the news.

Thus began the beating of breasts, some small, some large, some voluminous but not particularly erotic. There was great wailing, gnashing of teeth, and hair tearing. There was sackcloth and there were funeral pyres sending ash and soot into the skies over the cleanest state in the lower forty-eight. The outpouring marked the death of the two great icons of late twentieth century culture, Hunter S. Thompson and Sandra Dee. Both died on February 19, 2005, and half-mast flags flew above every courthouse, town hall, and post office, honoring the lives of these symbols of the great American cultural divide. One died from natural causes and the other, a large-gauge shotgun.

What better emblems of the culture wars than Sandra Dee and Hunter S. Thompson? Gidget on the beach never once letting that swimsuit slip, and Gonzo in a drunken drug rage in Las Vegas or wherever. Read Gonzo trying to understand what makes America tick via his own strange ticks; watch the sparky Dee oblivious to every tick that makes America tick.

Sandra Dee, or rather Alexandra Zuck, married Bobby Darin and they had a son, which means that Sandra was not the eternal virgin as her publicist claimed, unless the fetus was immaculately conceived. This is possible. Anything is possible. If a male inseminates a female the usual way, she could no longer be a virgin. But what if the male is a god? Gods do not have to use the standard method to inseminate women. It could be done with a shower of gold or a dropping from a supernatural pigeon. Then again, and much less magically, the technocrats of modern biological science fertilize in Petri dishes, and with the fertilized egg implanted, pregnancy is achieved, virginity maintained. But the technocrats were not ready to do that in the mid-sixties, unless one were bovine, so if Sandra Dee died a virgin, she did not have intercourse with Bobby Darin, and given their busy schedule, hectic and frenetic marriage, maybe she was inseminated by a god . . . . but which god? . . . and how do you do a paternity test on a god, anyway?

What of Hunter S. Thompson, Hunter Stockton Thompson, symbol of the wild, in your face side of life? Here was a walking study of how many legal, semi-legal, and simply illegal drugs and over-dosings of the same one can take without their having any long lasting effect on alcohol consumption. Sanity fails to be important when people believe they really are the President's fellow Americans, or believe that they have been wisely advised to think outside the box, achieve intimacy by bowling together, and to become ditto-heads. Here was the great counter-cultural hero, unveiling hypocrisy wherever he found it. How much outrage at the American dream does it take to reject the halls of Montezuma, the shores of Tripoli, Mr. Smith goes to Washington, while all the time leaping fat city skyscrapers and the ivy-covered towers of academia in a single bound? Better to pass time golfing with a Ruger semi-automatic 45 and fishing with an RPG.

Neither of these two Montana natives ever actually lived in Montana nor were they born there, but they probably would have if they had ever thought about it. Maybe they passed through on a skiing trip, or managed a *ménage à trois* while on a hunting or fishing expedition, or while white water rafting, or while they hung with Peter Fonda down in Paradise Valley, or something of that sort. But it sure felt like a favorite son and daughter had died, and that is all that counts. Besides, a lot people die who have never been to Montana, and Montanans have mourned for them too, except not as deeply.

So the funeral festivities for these two Montana natives was a mighty affair. Women with waist to hip ratios 6.8 to 7.2 flew in from Paris, New York, and Los Angeles. Kate Moss, and Naomi Campbell, and Marilyn Monroe, exhumed but looking as fresh as a daisy, were there. Leonardo DiCaprio, Mel Gibson, and Elvis Presley, who looked much better now that he dropped some of that weight, were there. It was like *Vanity Fair* had decided to go slumming with *People Magazine*. Donald Trump and Rumsfeld, Bill Gates, and Kofi Annan were present. Isn't that Eugenia Volodina, stunning Gucci model, with her arm around Red Fishburn? Her dress uniform smoky eye make-up is all tear-run, and Red's crying, too—so in touch with his feelings. C.D. Lukovich is similarly distraught. You do not find many men like that. There is Natalia Volodina being comforted by Hosanna Wright. Acting impresario Matthew Lunes, working from Pericles' famous funeral oration, had prepared a terrific eulogy. And it was all being taken down for the summer issue of *Foreign Affairs Journal*.

On a day filled with blond sunshine, Sandra Dee's nicely embalmed body was brought by a Greyhound bus entourage to the Great Falls Inter-Cosmological Space Port. It pulled past the main gate at the exact minute a Fed Ex agent arrived with a bucket filled with Hunter S. Thompson's ashes. In a ceremony that could only be described as both sentimentally solemn and commendably bizarre, the embalmed and the cremated were loaded into the nose cone of an ET23 Apollo Five rocket that Mrs. Goren's third graders had painted with very pretty lilies of the valley. *Beach Party Bingo* played across well-placed video screens and a dead ringer for Jerry Garcia sang,

> I come from Montana, I wear a bandana. My spurs are all silver,
> my pony is gray. While riding the ranges, my luck never changes.
> With foot in the stirrup, I gallop away.

At the end of the countdown, the rocket was to be fired into space on a trajectory that would have it circling the Earth for, whichever came first, an eternity or the Earth's collision with the sun.

The launch went perfectly and one more end of an era came as the end of an era swept across the plains and mountains of Montana. The wake was good, the funeral excellent, the interment splendid, and the mourning glorious. Soon it was February 26, St. Paddy's Day, so everybody went to Butte and got drunk.

And so is told one more new Montana absolutely real unreality.

MEET THE AUTHOR

Serena Sofia Flighfish settled in Montana in 1980, a full decade before Ted Turner, Peter Fonda, David Letterman, tourist agents, and travel magazines discovered the state.

Intelligent and vivacious, she has published sixty-five articles on Montana, Idaho, Wyoming, and the Dakotas. Her many books have been translated into numerous languages, including French, German, Spanish, Russian, Chinese, and Yiddish. The immensely successful *Lingerie Firecracker Stories* remains the definitive late twentieth century work of short fiction.

Serena was born in 1956 in Paris (her father, Harold Louis Flighfish, was the U.S. ambassador to France). At Columba University she was the recipient of the prestigious H. Abscurskii Fellowship, and while completing her studies at the Halvah School of Journalism, she was honored as the Phi Delta Kappa "Scholar of the Decade." After a several-year stint as fiction editor at the *Atlantis Monthly*, she moved to a rambling cottage on a mountainside near Helena with her aged mother, Anita Eve Flighfish-Sforza (Nobel Prize in physics, 1948).

Serena can often be seen fly-fishing at her favorite spot on the upper branch of the south fork of the Yellowstone River in her distinctive nylon waders and bustier. On off-days she continues her writing to the pleasure of her worldwide readership. *Montana: High Rise and Handsome* is Ms. Flighfish's refreshingly modern Montana mythology—a replacement for the worn-out fairytales in *The Last Best Place: A Montana Anthology* and Joseph Kinsey Howard's 1943 misguided epic, *Montana: High, Wide and Handsome.*